TWITCHER

WRITTEN AND ILLUSTRATED BY
KALEB SCHAD

TO HANNAH.
FOR BEING THERE. EVERY STEP. EVERY DAY.

I greatly appreciate you taking the time to read my work. Please consider leaving a review wherever you bought the book, or telling your friends about it, to help me spread the word.

Thank you so much for supporting my work.

www.kalebschadauthor.com

The text of this book is set in Adobe Caslon Pro.

GET THE
TWITCHER SKETCHBOOK
FOR FREE!

I love the chance to connect with readers. The very best way to do that is by joining my mailing list. You'll get early access to new releases, exclusive art, deleted scenes and sneak peeks at projects in development.

Details on how to sign up at the back of the book.

WHAT I CHOOSE IS MY CHOICE.
WHAT'S A BOY SUPPOSED TO DO?
THE KILLER IN ME IS THE KILLER IN YOU.

— Smashing Pumpkins, *Disarm*

A BOY

When sniping someone, especially with a two-hundred-year-old rifle like his Springfield .30-06, you have to consider a lot of factors that could reveal your position, noise being the first. That's why Tyler waited, miserable and wet in the corn field, to pull the trigger until the John Deere combine was next to him, swiveling it's thrusters vertical to land and begin threshing. His ears automatically dampened the crack of the shot by thirty decibels and the tendons and muscles of his shoulder were flooded with blood and proteins to increase elasticity, allowing the recoil to travel through his body without swinging the barrel off target. His Sakanaya Cybernetic left hand and forearm began a microscopic oscillation that mirrored that of the bullet rifling down the barrel so that as it exited, its trajectory was as true as any shot by a mortal in all of history. Tyler was just under two clicks out from the guard's station and at 850 meters per second, it would take over two seconds for the bullet to reach the man. A lifetime for Tyler. He felt the familiar boredom settle in as he waited.

The bullet passed through the guard's head, his blood and brains coughing out in a heated miasma visible only to Tyler's thermal sensors in his cybernetic right eye. The man's body crumpled.

Tyler worked the bolt action, caught the ejected shell, loaded a new one, then crouched, strapped on his backpack and began jogging toward the veterinarian clinic.

Agripharms weren't big clinics, usually a veterinarian, two or three technicians and a security guard. It didn't take any human effort to run the actual farms, only to dish out the meds and keep the livestock alive.

He swiped the dead guard's hand over the key pad and heard the door unlock.

Inside, he moved past the admin offices and their sleepless monitors blinking away the health of the livestock, up a set of stairs

into the dormitories. The faint filtered smell of cow shit colored the room. He moved like a sigh, gentle and quiet. He'd forgotten what it was like to do this, to be uninvited, afraid you'll be discovered, violence a possibility, a likelihood, if found.

Outside the veterinarian's door, Tyler paused. There were two other techs in rooms behind him. He knew they should all be under their synmaps, but what if they weren't? Was he prepared for what that would require?

He eased open the door and scanned the room. His right eye made a barely audible click as the aperture switched to near-infrared and the room's details came into focus. A woman lay in a cradle plugged into a synmap, the electrodes protruding from her hair like robotic porcupine quills, wires draped from the electrodes over the edges of the cradle to the synmap itself. An intravenous tube connected to her right arm. Her eyes twitched under their lids and she had a trace of white crust at the corners of her mouth, which was odd. Synmaps weren't supposed to arouse physiological responses, just mental simulations, but who knew what kind of smack she'd slung in her IV sack to ride along.

Next to her, in a cradle much too big for him, lay a boy no older than five. His head had been recently shaved with freshly installed synports, red tissue swollen around the edges. He had turned in the cradle and his head lolled off the edge like he was going to fall.

Tyler stood over the woman. Watching her while scoping this place over the last several weeks, he knew she was a kind woman who treated her son well, but to get what he wanted, he needed her to be afraid of him. Tyler seized the electrodes and yanked. There was a wet popping sound as the couplers released, the slurp of needles retracting from her brain, and then there was her scream. She rolled out of her cradle, thrashing on the floor, wailing. Was her anguish from pain or because she was pulled out of whatever bullshit story she'd been living?

"Thetabiencort," Tyler said when she'd stopped to catch her breath.

"Wh-." She huddled on all fours, rubbing at her eyes. She'd dyed her nails an iridescent pink that blinked a random pattern in the dark.

"I need your thetabiencort. You need to unlock the fridge."

She was coming to grips, a frightening reality gelling around her. "Who are you?"

Tyler tapped his watch. "Lady, I don't have time. Open the fridge or I kill you and get the next tech to do it."

Tyler followed her out of her quarters, down two sets of stairs into a lab. She leaned on the railing, a hand probing her scalp for blood. Everything was stainless steel and cold. She stumbled to the vault and began keying her entry code.

"How did you even get out of the city? If you need a hit of something, just use your portion like everyone else," she said.

The door unlocked, a metallic thump of giant bolts retracting, and a cloud of frost pillowed out from the broken seal. Tyler stopped her from entering, told her to kneel with her hands behind her back and forehead on the floor. He went into the cooler and followed her directions to the thetabiencort. It was a liquid in small metal canisters with the Staern Life Sciences logo etched across the surface.

Staern Life Sciences. SLS. The company that had made him what he was, that had wired his body with wretched narcotics and mechanical bits so thoroughly that he would die within years. Turned him into a dead man walking. Even gave him a watch so he could count to the second how much life he had left. It felt fitting that Tyler would now use one last narcotic from them to truly, finally end that life they had already stolen six years ago.

He shoveled the entire shelf into his backpack.

Back in her quarters he had the tech lay on her cradle. Now what? He couldn't let her go, obviously. She couldn't go back under the synmap, not with how he ripped them out like that. Probably wouldn't be able to for weeks. He knew he should kill her. Would have killed her two years ago.

He walked next to her and leaned over.

She sucked in a shaking breath. "No," she said. "Don't."

He knew how he looked to her. Years of wilderness clawed into his skin. His reddish orange beard and mustache making him look older than the twenty-seven he was. Red. As if his cheeks and chin were burning. As if he had been bobbing for apples in Hell and the flames had stuck. Tyler reached across her and used the loose synmap cords to tie her left wrist. As he worked on her right wrist, he saw her looking at the carbon fiber carotids running up his neck under his jaw.

"You're a JACKK?"

Tyler moved to her legs.

"Why would they send you here? What is this?"

With her tied, Tyler straightened and looked at the boy. He was further off of his cradle now, one arm dangling. Tyler had watched the woman play with this boy in the yard. He seemed like a decent kid, obedient and joyful. Sometimes she would bring out a baby goat and they'd play with it for a while. The kid seemed to like that.

Tyler went to the boy sliding off of his cradle.

"Don't wake him," the woman said. "Please. He just got the ports, if you wake him now he'll never go back under. You realize how long I've waited for the little shit to start sleeping like a normal person?"

Her words churned in Tyler. He should have known. It was all bullshit, the games he had seen her playing with the child. Just wasting time until the synports could be installed.

He eased the child back onto his cradle.

She watched Tyler pick up his backpack, the thetabiencort clinking inside, her eyes following him to the door.

"If you shoot that theta you'll die," she said. "It'll kill you. Even you."

Tyler looked at his watch. Minus 06 days, 19 hours, 44 minutes and 23 seconds.

"I'm counting on it," he said.

Voices first.

"Is he dead?"

"Ben, hurry."

A boy and a man. The man had an accent.

"I think he was a doctor. These are doctor books."

"Blankets, Ben. Boots, warm clothes, whatever you can find."

The boy was next to Tyler.

"Look at all of the blood."

"It's from that machine. He's going to wake up, Ben, hurry."

Tyler's Sakanaya eye cycled on while he kept his flesh eye closed and lay still. He remembered sitting down to start dialysis. His face was laying in something wet and now he could see flashlight beams tumbling around the room. His dialysis machine lay shattered on its side, the outflow tube missing and blood sprayed everywhere. A seizure. He must have had another.

His Sakanaya switched to night vision.

"Is that his gun?"

"Ben." The man took three thumping steps toward the boy. Tyler snaked out his hand and caught the man's ankle, sweeping his feet out from under him.

The boy screamed and tried to jump away, but slipped in the blood and flopped backwards, thwacking his head on the floor. His flashlight spun away, strobing the room.

The man landed hard. He tried to scramble, but Tyler was faster. Always faster. He climbed on top of the man's back, grabbed him by the hair and drove his face into the wooden floor so hard the floorboards bucked. He rolled the man onto his back and punched him twice, the first breaking his cheekbone, the second finishing off his nose. He could feel his JACKK pumping. Tyler had to remind himself to pull his punches, forgetting how strong he was—how weak normals were.

Tyler held his third punch like an asteroid waiting to fall. The man had a dark brown beard and mustache, red sacks around his eyes, the sign of a man exhausted or coming off of something, aching for a hit of Seven Ten or emenethol or anything. Tyler would know. Had seen it enough times in the mirror in his earlier years.

Both the man and the boy were covered in mud and scratches and their hair hugged their scalps like it had been hidden under hats for days without washing or sunlight.

"Three words or less. Why are you here?"

The man moved his lips as he counted, finally deciding on, "Hungry and cold."

"Please, mister, don't hurt Eddie," the boy said. "We saw your cabin. We thought you were dead." The boy wore an orange jumpsuit that had the SLS logo of Staern Life Sciences on it. He was young, not quite a teenager, not quite a little kid, maybe eleven, with blond hair, soft cheeks and unguarded eyes.

Tyler stood up, put a foot on the man's cheek and smashed his face sideways as he leaned to grab his .30-06 resting against the wall behind him. Tyler saw his Mark 9 handgun was on the table three meters away along with two clips. How long had he been out? He hadn't left that gun there.

"Were you sneaking down from the — shut up," Tyler said. Outside. He heard a jeep ease to a stop and shut down, hydraulics lowering a suspension system. That meant military or industrial.

Tyler worked the action on the .30-06 and drove a shell into the receiver, appreciating the look on Eddie's face as he did so. Today's guns just didn't have that murderous crack of metal on metal when a round was chambered.

He pointed the gun at Eddie's right eye. "You have friends?"

"What?"

"Outside."

The boy whispered, "They followed us."

"Please," Eddie said. "They want Ben. They'll kill you and me and take him."

"Maybe you two. Kid, kill the light," Tyler said, unaware of how right he was.

He stepped over Eddie so he had line-of-action to his cabin's door. Two years and the only soul that had crossed that threshold was his own, whatever kind of soul it was. Now, six days from the end, this shit happens.

Tyler heard them step onto the porch, one man sneaking around to the window over the sink, the other three waiting. Then, without speaking, which meant hand signals or comms implants — either way, probably military — they breached the door. A red laser sliced through the archaic hinges Tyler had used when building the place and the door collapsed in. He hadn't planned on defending himself against the LCP armed forces, would have built a sterner door.

They rushed the room, the front two soldiers barking for Tyler to get down, to drop the gun, to get back, none of which Tyler would do. The first soldier stopped at the end of the hall and pointed the beam former of a Ranzel L226 personal laser system at Tyler, the power conduit slinking around to the backpack. The second zeroed in on the boy like a shark after blood. The first soldier screamed at Tyler a second time to get down. Drop the fucking gun.

Tyler stepped back from Eddie, but held the gun over his head in one hand.

A third man in a civilian uniform walked up and patted at the walls in the hallway. "Don't you have any lights in here?" He wore glasses, a pointless affectation for the past that some High Laners had, and his uniform had the SLS logo on it. Staern Life Sciences again. Just when you thought you were done with them, that they couldn't ruin anything else…but Tyler should have known better. After all, he still had six days to live, didn't he? And if there was one thing SLS was good at, it was fucking up Tyler's life.

The soldiers wore standard tactical gear—tactical shirt and pants, armored vest, Sakanaya implants for both, sync cables for their weapons snaking out of the synports in their scalp—though their uniforms also had SLS logos on them, not the Liberty Conglomerate Province government badge Tyler had expected.

The second soldier threw the boy to his stomach and knelt on his back.

A merciless blue light filled the cabin and the third man said, "Better." He looked at the boy and Eddie, then at Tyler, assessing the blood. "Holy hell. They did a number on you."

"It's not mine," Tyler said. "Well, it is, but not from them."

"Leave us alone," the boy groaned from under the soldier.

"We're not supposed to let you talk," Glasses said, then to the second soldier with the rifle, "If he speaks again, make him wish he hadn't."

"He's just a boy," Eddie said. "He doesn't deserve this."

"He's no more a boy, than this laser is a flashlight," the first soldier said.

"You did good. Eddie, is it?" The man took off his glasses and cleaned them, as if he'd seen it in a syncast and thought it looked sophisticated. Before they left this cabin, Tyler was going to make that man eat those glasses. "All the way through Ottawa, up between the lakes and back down to here. That's what? Two-thousand kilometers?"

"One-thousand nine-hundred thirty-six," said the first soldier. He hadn't looked away from Tyler yet, but he'd let the beam former droop under the weight.

"He's just a boy," Eddie said again, this time tired. This time like he was trying to convince himself. How easy giving up was.

The boy began to plead as he was hauled to his feet. Don't. I'm sorry. I'm not what you think I am. The soldier punched the kid in the gut, sending his breath and courage fleeing.

Tyler took a half-step and Laser Dick lifted the beam former.

Glasses said, "He's a Cull. SLS property."

Cull. Cullings. The word bombarded Tyler. A child. His mother behind him. Flash of fire and two small piles of ash. Two dust piles of life. Tens of thousands of dust piles.

"Okay," Glasses said, reeling Tyler back. "Let's clean the room."

"Now, hold on," Tyler said.

"Brooks," Laser Dick said. He gestured with the laser. "Look."

Glasses looked at Tyler and he watched as the man's eyes traveled from Tyler's face to his neck, to the carbon fiber carotids inserting under his jaw, to the too-dark veins bulging in his forearms, to the iconic watch.

He opened his mouth, then closed it. After a moment: "You're a Twitcher?"

"I never liked that term," Tyler said.

"Oh God," Eddie moaned.

"Why are you—"

"Please, mister," the boy said.

"You called him a Cull." Even saying the word was hard. The once-a-decade government-ordered Depopulation Protocol. For the no-bullshitters in the room: slaughter. But don't worry. It's all in the name of a greater good. Generations of Lower Skimmers sacrificing their lives in defense against the Resource Gap. If you force someone to die for something, is that still a sacrifice? From where Tyler had been standing it looked more like murder, but, you know, tomayto, tomahto.

He'd spent his entire childhood having nightmares of being Culled. Then, courtesy of Staern Life Sciences, he lived the nightmare.

"This boy is SLS property, like you," Glasses said. "It's important that you not get involved."

"LCP police or military do Cullings."

"They do. Did. How long have you been out here?"

Tyler didn't answer.

"We're developing new ways of handling Cullings that are less invasive."

"Less invasive."

"Less overt, let's say."

"But still Culling," Tyler said. "Still killing people."

"Technically, the courts ruled they aren't."

"People."

"Technically."

Something was stoked within Tyler, an ember he'd forgotten, thought had burned out two years ago in Liberty Heights under that residence tower, but now threatened to conflate into something uncontrollable. For two years he had hidden out here, desperate to feel nothing, to remember nothing, but these men and child had brought something to him better than buried feelings. They had brought him back his rage.

"You fuckers haven't changed at all," he said.

No more a child than that laser is a flashlight, they said. A tool. And what was a tool in the hands of a man, but a way to destroy something? Tyler was good at destroying things. If there was anything he was good at, it was that.

"I never liked the 226," Tyler said to the soldier holding the laser.

"No?" The soldier's eyes settled as he said it, as if he knew a decision had been made, as if he knew the outcome of that decision and regretted it. Maybe one had. Maybe he should.

"Too heavy. I like being able to move."

"You seem more of an antique guy. Old fashioned, maybe," Laser Dick said.

"Two years, four months, twenty-three days, sixteen hours and," Tyler looked at his watch, "four seconds. Give or take."

"Okay?" Glasses said.

"You asked how long I've been out here. I haven't dealt with a single other person in all that time. It was nice." Tyler looked at the boy and Eddie, then back to Glasses. "And I'm nobody's property."

He threw his .30-06 at Laser Dick's face. It's called the startle pattern and every mammal does it. It's a genetic reflex to danger. With Tyler's enhanced perception, time slowed and he watched as Laser Dick swiveled his head in slow motion to the gun arcing through the air, his arms pulling in towards his body, legs bending. Meanwhile, Tyler was moving off-center and forward.

There are three rules to successful close-quarters combat: surprise, speed and violence-of-action. Tyler was built for all three. He reached Laser Dick at the same time the Springfield did, knocked down the L226 with his left hand, flattened out his right one and drove it through the man's throat nearly taking off his head. The Springfield crashed into Laser Dick's dead face. Tyler snatched it out of the air by the barrel.

He paused, letting Glasses catch up, to recognize what was happening. When Tyler saw clarity come across the man's face, he said, "I like the glasses." He used the rifle as a baseball bat, driving the glasses and the man's face into the back of his own skull, popping his head like a balloon filled with crimson mud.

Eddie was on his feet and running toward the table, reaching for the MK-9. The window in the kitchen melted, then splintered as the soldier outside fired his laser. It sliced through Eddie's side, releasing a pungent smell of burning cotton and flesh.

"Eddie," the boy screamed. He tried to buck his hips to get the soldier off of him, but was out of his weight class by sixty kilos.

If the soldier on Ben was any good, Tyler knew, he'd shoot at Tyler and ignore Eddie. Focus on the primary threat. Tyler dropped his rifle, leapt towards the last soldier. The soldier pivoted on his knee and sprayed his assault rifle at Tyler in a desperate, stuttering arc. Tyler planted a foot on the wall next to him and swan dived over the spray of bullets. His perception was enhanced enough to see the bounce of the muzzle after each flash, to time the next shot and calculate what its deviation from the target would be in plus or minus degrees above and below sight line. He knew he was above that range.

The bullets sizzled as they passed under Tyler, the sound of the shot milliseconds behind it. Then Tyler was on the soldier and grabbing his head in both hands and twisting. Dry twigs in late summer would have given more resistance.

The kitchen window lit up again, but the shot went wide of Tyler, searing through the far wall. He scooped up his .30-06, raced out the door, banked right, tossed the Springfield to his left hand, swung it around the edge of the cabin and pulled the trigger. That fast. One motion. There was a sacrilegious flash and roar of the gun in the forest night. He heard the man on the porch grunt. Tyler rounded the corner, dragged the man off of the porch by the pack's straps, then used the soldier's own laser to slice off his head.

Tyler looked at the decapitated man. Steam from the blood twirled in the moon's callous light.

What had he done? These weren't vet tech rent-a-cops. Malcolm

Staern and SLS didn't let people like this disappear. Tyler should know.

"Fuck me," he whispered.

Six days and change. He could have let them take whoever these twats in his cabin were and hoped it took seven days for SLS to send more folks out to check on the Twitcher in the woods. By then, it wouldn't have mattered. But, no, he had to go kill everyone and ruin it all. If there was one thing Tyler was good at, it was destroying things.

Eddie was going to die, that much was clear. The laser had burned through his lung and into the upper colon at the least, probably through the descending colon and some of the small intestine as well. There wasn't a lot of blood, the laser cauterizing much of it, but the damage was fatal.

The boy was kneeling next to Eddie, holding his hand, crying.

"Take him," Eddie said when he saw Tyler standing over him. "Out of the LCP."

"What do they mean he's a Cull?"

"They won't stop."

"How is the boy a Cull? What does that mean?"

"Please, mister," the boy said. "Help him."

"They took him. It wasn't his fault."

"How does he work?" Tyler nudged Eddie with his boot. Shock was sucking the man's consciousness away.

"You're a doctor. Why won't you help him?"

"I don't know," Eddie said. "Quietly. It wasn't his fault."

"You have doctor books!"

"It wasn't his fault." Eddie slurped a breath.

"Staern Life Sciences made him?"

"Just a boy."

"Malcolm Staern?"

"Eddie," the boy cried. He shook Eddie's shoulder.

Staern had stuck this kit in Tyler's body. Not Staern himself, of course, but his company. His defense division that partnered with the Liberty Conglomerate Province military. Live fast. Die fast. Tyler couldn't say they weren't honest with him, but what choice did he have? What choice was left to him? They knew that, too. What choice had they left him?

And wasn't that the story of his fucking life? Never given a choice, always things done to him until Tyler thought the doing couldn't get any worse and then it did. Every time. Hey kid, give me your Seven Ten, his mom would say, making it near impossible for Tyler to go back under the synmap. When he ran away from home and met the Red Lithiums and thought he had found a real family, of people awake and living with each other, he thought this was it, this was the place he would die happy. Well, they tried for the first half of that, not much caring about the second half. Of course LCP wasn't interested in a boy running for his life, no cubit to live in, not even on the dole anymore. Deceased, they said. It says so right here. Deceased. Five years ago, age eight. Fucking government. Street life it was, then. By the time Staern's 'cruiters found him, he hadn't eaten in weeks and had allowed…Tyler wouldn't let himself remember any more. But he sure as shit remembered how it started. Who started it all.

He looked at his watch. -06:03:19:33.

"How did you get through Cerebus Gate North? How did you get out of the city?"

Six days. If they drove, they could retrace Eddie's path and reach the northern gate to Elia in a day and a half. Through Elia to the center of the city in another day and a half, maybe two. Be at Staern Life Sciences tower in three, maybe four days total. What was he considering?

The boy ran to the kitchen where a towel lay crumpled next to the sink. He shook out the broken glass, small bells in the steel basin.

"How did you get through the gate?"

Eddie's head lolled.

The boy knelt and pressed the towel to Eddie's side, trying to staunch what little blood there was.

"The gate, Eddie. They don't just let you through. How did you get through?" He shoved Eddie with his boot again, harder.

"Stop it," the boy shouted.

They did this to him. Tyler didn't give a shit about the man —

had never met him before today—but it was the principle of it. They had a "Me first and to Hell with everyone else" attitude that had decimated Tyler's and his mother's lives. The things they had made him do... By God, six days might be enough time.

Eddie opened his mouth, but only blood instead of words.

"Help him," the boy cried.

"Yeah," Tyler said. He walked over to the table, picked up his Mark 9 and racked the slide.

"Stop. No!"

Tyler returned to the man, pointed the gun at Eddie's temple and pulled the trigger.

That was the last thing Tyler would do for another person. From here on, Tyler was doing something for himself. This Cull-kid looked to be the perfect parting gift from this boot-shit world. An apology dropped in his lap. Tyler would take the apology and shove it down Staern's throat. Make it go boom.

Laser Dick looked to be about the right size and his uniform hadn't been shot through. The blood and little bit of bone on the collar could be rinsed out. Anyway the uniform was black. Maybe this could be their way through Cerebus North.

The kid had skidded back when Tyler shot Eddie, but blood had gotten on him anyway. Tyler could see he was rattling hard, volts of terror trembling through him.

"Take off your clothes," Tyler said.

The boy didn't move.

"Kid." Tyler took a step towards him and the boy looked up. "Strip."

"Why?"

Tyler leaned down and pulled at the kid's collar, catapulting him to his feet.

The boy unzipped his SLS jumpsuit. Once he was naked, Tyler walked around the boy examining every pale centimeter of flesh, lifting his arms, combing his fingers through the boy's hair, lifting his eyelids. No scars. No implants except the synports on his scalp and the fistula in his left arm that everyone got. Clean.

"Anything in you?"

"What?"

"Tracers, 'netics. Bombs."

The boy looked at Tyler.

"Get dressed," Tyler said.

Tyler's Mark 37 assault rifle from back when he was an official soldier of the LCP Corporate Assault Forces and eleven magazines of high-powered, self-guided rounds. His MK-9 pistol and six twenty-round magazines of splatter rounds. Two E15 incendiary grenades. The Springfield and his last four shells for it. His old combat vest that still smelled like Chicago. A Melmoth combat shirt made from LV that combined flexible, laser dispersing and ballistic retarding fibers. Still heavy, but helpful when the shit hits the fan. Inside his rucksack: a change of socks, underwear and a t-shirt, his TX armor-piercing knife, a hard case kit that held his multi-tool, tape, rope, tourniquet and ferro cerium rod. A thermal blanket that reflected back his heat for warmth and masked his heat signature from thermal detection. An AnyAqua thermos with self-cleansing filtration liner. Makes piss taste like Canadian spring water. A cell-powered chainsaw and gloves. Eddie Fahrs's credit chip with thirty-thousand chips on it. A stainless steel plunger of amphetamine boosters and blood dopers.

And the thetabiencort. Just in case.

These were the things he put in his Light Tactical Vehicle, silent and heavy. In life, often, there is a weight to waiting, a burdensome purposelessness that is undetectable. It wasn't until Tyler had loaded his vehicle, the accoutrements of revenge — murder? Did it matter? — stowed, that he felt the lightness of decision. Of purpose.

These were the things he put in his jeep. These things and a weapon in the shape of a boy.

Tyler kept to the old roads from before the Great Divestment, but that meant some rough riding over crumbling asphalt and gravel trails. So far he'd only had to stop twice to use the chainsaw and clear trees. As dawn broke, Tyler could see buzzing across the horizon combines and fertilizers, harvesters and feed bots and sprinklers, a bee's colony of automated agriculture wrapping up the fall harvest and fertilizing fields before winter. He knew he could drive a thousand miles and as long as he avoided the few agripharms between here and there, he wouldn't see another human being until he reached Cerebus Gate North.

The blinking lights on wingtips and tail rotors reminded him of fireflies in June bobbing above the grass behind his cabin and he thought about how he would never see them again. He checked his watch: -05:17:58:12.

"Why does it count backwards," the boy asked.

Tyler curled forward like a cat and stretched his back.

"Your watch. Why does it count backwards?"

"It's counting my time left," Tyler said. "Shut up."

"Time left until what?"

Here and there, the sideways sunlight skipped across crumbled silos and farms. A flock of turkeys—was that right? Flock? Tyler thought he'd learned a different word.—scurried off the road in front of them and into the brush.

"I'm hungry," the boy said.

Of course. Tyler was an idiot. How could he have forgotten food for the kid? He had to eat so rarely, himself, it wasn't part of his readiness routine.

"The human body can go more than three weeks without food. You'll be fine."

"Three weeks? That's a long time. Are you a doctor? Is that why you had doctor books?"

Maybe if he didn't answer the kid would shut up.

"You don't look like a doctor. You're too big. What are those thingies on your arm and neck?"

"Kid. Shut up." Tyler needed to think. He needed a plan to get through Cerebus Gate North if the uniforms didn't do it. Last time he'd snuck through there'd been so much chaos what with the tower collapsing and the military operating in and out of the gate, worried the tower had dropped from an attack from the Midlands.

Cerebus North.

Liberty Heights.

A residence tower filled with tens of thousands of people under synmaps, but not all of them. Some of them were awake on their scheduled relapse. Some of them were in the kitchens preparing solid foods instead of the nutrient sacs they'd lived on for the last ten days while they were under. Some of them were warned of what was coming before they'd felt it.

"I don't want to go three weeks," the boy said.

Tyler returned to the jeep.

"Without eating," the boy said.

"You won't have to. Three, four days, max."

"Why? Where are you taking me?"

What difference did it make if the boy knew? Tyler knew when—to the second — he was going to die. Shouldn't the boy?

"I'm taking you back. We're going to figure out what makes you go boom and then we're going to walk into Malcolm Staern's tower and do just that."

"That's not what I do."

"You're a Cull, aren't you?"

"I'm a Ben."

"You're a weapon."

"Stop it."

"See these?" Tyler pulled back his sleeve and shoved his forearm in front of the kid's face, squeezing a fist, revealing corded muscles and deep purple JACKK veins. "It's called the Joint Auto-pharmaceutical and Cybernetic Kinesis Kit. Only the best in amphetamines, antipsychotics, steroids and nanocellotics that science can imagine. The same guy who made you put this shit in me."

"Stop it."

"And for the same reason."

"Shut up!" The boy started crying.

"We're not so different, you and I," Tyler said. "Both killers."

The sun crawled skyward and as they passed the northern corner of Lake Huron, Tyler could see the skeletons of ships crusted into the shorelines, masts standing like gravestones. From a time when people did such things as sailing and fishing. Now nobody sailed and anyone could sail, with the right syncast.

Eventually the boy had stopped crying and watched the

countryside. "We could stay here. Or go back to your cabin."

This again.

"You're dying. That's what your watch is counting, right? We could go back to your cabin and I could stay with you and we could play games or tell stories and when you weren't feeling good I could make you something and I could try and help you."

Tyler didn't answer.

"Where are your friends?"

"They train you to talk so much?"

"I had lots of friends. They made me. When I came out for relapses. They'd ask me if I wanted to go and make friends."

"You're not a Skimmer, are you? Skimmers don't have friends."

"None? Who do they play with?"

"And anyway, the only friends I ever had tried to kill me. Hell, everyone ever has."

The kid didn't say anything for a long time and Tyler thought maybe he'd gotten bored and wasn't paying attention anymore, but when he looked at the boy, when he saw the boy was staring at him, but not seeing him, Tyler knew he'd nicked something deep.

"Why'd you say that?" the boy whispered.

"What?"

"I didn't."

"Didn't what?"

"Eric asked to see his mom and dad and I told Mrs. Kathy that he didn't want to play anymore and she said she would take him home and that they would make him feel better before he left and, anyway, it wasn't me. I was just there with him. He got sick by himself." It was as if the words vomited up from somewhere the boy hadn't known existed within himself and this sudden knowledge of guilt terrified the child as much as the secret itself. He breathed hard through his nose.

The jeep hunched up and down as it climbed over a mostly rotted tree stump.

"Huh," Tyler said.

Why would they do that? Why would they give their weapon emotions and guilt? It seemed an extra ounce of cruel. One more reason to kill every one of those bastards.

After a while Tyler leaned over the steering wheel and said, "Well, anyway, this is important."

"Why? Blowing up a building won't matter."

"It will when Staern himself is in it."

"Why?"

"Because I said so." Isn't that what parents would tell their kids in the syncasts?

"But why?"

Tyler would be damned if he was going to play confessional with an eleven year old murder machine made by Staern, but he needed the kid to shut up so he could think. "Because I'm dying at twenty-seven and because of the shit he put me through and made me do. Now, enough!"

"Maybe you could make a syncast. Give it to those other people who don't like the government and are putting out syncasts all the time."

Tyler didn't know what "other people" the kid was talking about, nor did he care.

"Stop, please," the boy said. "Just stop so we can talk."

Tyler pressed the accelerator.

"Why won't you stop?" The boy was nearly screaming now. "Why aren't you doing what I say?"

Tyler felt dizzy, seeing the world as if through heated air, flapping and false. The kid reached over and grabbed the steering wheel and tried to pull it. With the back of his hand, Tyler slapped the boy's mouth, knocking him into the headrest, then slammed on the brakes. The kid plunged forward, catching himself on the dash.

"Look at me," Tyler yelled. "Look at me. If you want to get to Elia with your tongue, you will shut up. And if you want to get to Elia with your hands, you will never, ever, until the day you die, touch me or this steering wheel again."

The boy licked at his cut lip, turned and spit out the side of the jeep.

Tyler looked at his watch. His countdown showed a half hour had passed, but it had only been fifteen minutes since he'd last checked. Somehow he'd lost an extra fifteen minutes. That had only ever happened after a gunfight or a mission, whenever his JACKK had fired full-tilt in his blood stream. Was this how it was going to go from here on? Was his survival time going to lose sync with chronological time? Was his lifespan shorter than he'd thought? It was unnerving. For six years he had lived with a certainty of death, but to the minute, the second. A tradeoff in knowledge, ambiguous to certain.

The boy looked at Tyler, then out the side of the jeep at the infinite and lifeless lake and said, "I am nothing like you."

Resignation and exhaustion eventually won and the boy slept. He rested his head on the roll bar and his mouth sagged in a pout. It gave the little shit a look of innocence, as if he were truly a boy and nothing more. But isn't that how they worked? Cover their violence in candy? Narcotics by the bagful to make you feel. Stories fired into your brain, electrocuting you with emotion. Stories that helped you escape what is with what isn't.

The boy was no more innocent than Tyler. He told himself this. Maybe he believed it.

They drove all through that day watching the hills rise up and drop away, the decades-old asphalt and concrete destroyed by things like poplar trees and switchgrass. Every now and then they passed farms long abandoned and growing nothing but memories of a time when people lived outside of the cities, brick silos crumbled and hollow, their roofs pockmarked with shadowed holes. Stone skeletons standing like broken teeth.

How was he going to get through Cerebus Gate North with this tumor in tow? He had the uniforms and the ID chip, but what if they weren't enough? Would the kid run when Tyler said to? Would he try and get Tyler killed?

He looked back at the road and there were two of them, doubled and dancing. Tyler squeezed his eye closed and opened it again, somewhat useless because the Sakanaya never turned off, but it didn't help anyway. He shook his head, but that was a mistake. Tingling sparked down his arms and legs and then he knew. A seizure.

"What," the boy said, the sway of the jeep waking him.

Tyler tried to get his foot off of the accelerator, over to the brake, but it was too late.

His neck hurt. The jeep was on its side ten meters away, its undercarriage and chassis exposed to him like looking up a woman's skirt. He could see a black lump that he thought might be his backpack another thirty meters behind the vehicle. Tyler swore to himself. The boy.

Circling the jeep, he tried to prepare for what he would find. Prepare for a mission failed. Instead he found it empty. Tyler looked around, scanning with his Sakanaya at seven power for any movement, thermal for heat signatures. Nothing. He did see his .30-06 a couple meters away. He went to it and picked it up and then he noticed his sidearm was missing from his holster, the flap unbuckled. That wouldn't happen. Not by itself.

If it began to rain, as the sky was threatening, he'd have a harder time finding the boy, any tracks being washed away. He moved out from the jeep in widening concentric circles, looking for footprints or blood and found both on the third loop, moving into a field. Six hundred meters in he saw the boy crouching in the grasses, his orange jumpsuit blazing like a beacon. What an idiot. His enhanced hearing could hear the boy whispering to himself, a kind of prayer over and over. Don't find me. Don't find me.

When it was obvious Tyler had indeed found him, the boy sat up and pointed the MK-9. He had a cut on his forehead and blood had painted half of his face.

"I don't want to—"

"Give me the gun."

"But I will."

"Kid, I'm hurt and we're wasting time."

"Just let me go. Leave me here."

"A pistol and a jumpsuit? That's what you think you'll need? And who the hell hides in a grass field wearing an orange jumpsuit?"

"You can kill Mr. Staern by yourself. You don't need me."

Tyler craned his neck, trying to loosen whatever he'd done to it in the accident, when he saw the doe. She was big, standing at the edge of the field a hundred meters out and she was watching them, her ears swiveled forwards, tail swishing once or twice.

Tyler raised the rifle slowly, slowly, pointing it over the boy's head. "Don't move," he whispered.

The doe blew at him, a weird trumpeting sound, like a man with a sinus infection, and Tyler fired. She crouched, then bound forward two or three leaps before her front legs crumpled and she drove into the dirt, her hind quarters somersaulting over her head.

The boy had turned to see what Tyler was aiming at and when he turned back, Tyler was standing in front of him, taking the MK-9 from his hands.

"You said you were hungry," Tyler said.

She was a good whitetail, plenty of meat for the next couple of days as long as Tyler could keep her cool. The autumn air would help with that. He rolled her on her back, kneeled on her hind legs and flipped out his knife.

Thick, but scattered, raindrops began to fall. A precursor to a pouring.

"You shot it," the boy said.

Tyler cut away the teats to clear the belly, then sawed around the anus to release the muscles and tendons. He could tell the boy was both fascinated and frightened.

"That's the problem," Tyler said as he worked. He was using a combination of the knife and his fingers to separate the organs from the stomach muscles now, careful not to puncture the guts and poison the meat. "People don't have a sense of the world. They spend their days under a synmap, getting their nutrients by a drip, or if they're awake and eating solids, they don't ask or think about where the food comes from." Tyler crunched the knife up the sternum, breaking the ribs. "Everything is bullshit. They tell Skimmers stories of the great sacrifice they make during Cullings. You go under, experience the syncast, you get an extra dose of Seven Ten in your IV and you cry at how heroic and beautiful it all is." By now Tyler's arms were buried elbow deep up the deer's neck. The sharp bones of the ribs, clawed at his forearms. He grabbed the ridged esophagus, slippery, and with the knife in his other hand severed it.

"Okay, grab the front legs," he said.

The boy didn't move.

"The front legs. Grab them."

Startling forward, the boy tripped on the deer's snout as he tried to straddle the head and fell into Tyler.

"Dammit, kid, just grab the legs and lift."

The boy scrambled back to his feet, the deer's blood streaked across his jumpsuit, and he grabbed the front hooves.

Tyler stood and walked backwards, pulling the esophagus. All of the organs and entrails poured out of the deer onto the grass and the copper smell of blood and shit stewed in the rain. All of the things that once made a life now a pile of stink and slop.

"That is where your food comes from," Tyler said. "And that," he nudged the gut pile with his boot, "is the cost of living. Something else must die."

It turned out that getting the tactical vehicle back on its wheels was an easier task than getting it out of the ditch. Tyler had the boy sit in the driver's seat and told him to press the accelerator when he said go, then stop once on the road. Don't overshoot it and end up in the ditch on the other side, he'd warned. After pushing and grunting, his feet skidding out in the mud, the engine impotently roaring, he realized the kid was pressing both the brake and the accelerator.

"I've never driven," the boy said. "I've never done anything."

Nine hours later they laid under a decomposing barn roof, slanted and wrong, listening to the rain ping against the sheet metal. Two walls were now piles of gravel, catching the skidding rain in pools. Tyler could still smell the smoke from their smoldering fire, the roasted venison. He had taken off his belt rig with his ammo so he could stretch out. Tyler figured they were at most twelve hours out from Cerebus and he wanted to go into that situation rested.

Looking at his watch, -04:20:16:31, he knew healing after the accident had eaten ten extra hours off of his life. He'd need to watch that. He'd always lost time when his JACKK worked, but it had never been that drastic. All signs of the end, he knew.

After a long while of listening to the paper sounds of leaves under rain, the boy asked, "Why'd they go?"

"Who?"

"The people who made this barn?"

"They didn't. They died. Go to sleep."

He could tell the boy wanted to ask how, but didn't want to get yelled at, so he kept silent. Then the boy rammed up straight when a coyote let out its *yip yooowwww* cry eighty or a hundred meters out. It's siblings caught on quick, singing the chorus.

"What is that?" The kid whispered it.

"You didn't hear coyotes all that way out here?"

The boy shook his head.

"Go to sleep. They're hunting. They'll leave us alone. We're moving in three hours, so sleep. Now."

The kid was shivering and Tyler didn't think it was from the October cold. Ten minutes later, maybe when the kid thought Tyler was asleep already, he first heard, then felt the boy slide across the gravel and press up against him. The kid clasped his hands under his chin and pressed his face into Tyler's back.

He stopped shivering.

By mid-morning the next day, the rain had stopped and they could see Cerebus Gate North and the wall. It spanned northeast to southwest as far as the Earth's curve would reveal. A river of concrete and steel. A desperate hand keeping out the Midwestern crazies in what used to be the plain states and central Canada, keeping in the urban crazies in the Lower Skims. But a wall is only as strong as the gates through it and the Cerebus Gates were powerful. Seven levels of traffic entered under constant threat of destruction. Gunships hovered and scanned vehicles—almost all of which were piloted by automated systems—escorting them, blessing them.

Tyler watched the traffic, the security, and he felt a flittering under his stomach he hadn't felt in years. He was one man. This was the entire Liberty Conglomerate Province and the combined strength of the Big Seven. All of their money. All of their authority.

Was he really going to do this alone?

"I didn't get to see it last time," the boy said. "It's big."

Tyler pulled the SLS uniform out of his bag and began to strip. "We're going through on the bottom level." He talked while he dressed. "They're going to scan my jeep. If we're lucky, the SLS chip gets us through and nobody gets hurt, but if we're not, the AI will route us to security. If that happens, you do what I say, when I say. Move when I move. I want you to be the tumor you are and stick to me. Understand?"

The boy didn't look at him, but only stared at the wall.

Tyler turned the boy towards him. "If I get even a whiff that you are trying something or if it looks like we aren't going to make it through, I will put a bullet right here." He jabbed the boy above his left eye. "Understand? Tell me you understand."

"We don't have to go. Once we go in there, we can't go back. We can still go back."

Tyler buckled his tactical vest over the melmoth shirt. A click. Crisp. Final.

He held a deep breath, then let it out and said, "Retreat forward, kid."

Sitting there, waiting, surrounded by automated semis, logging trucks and tankers, smelling the wet asphalt, Tyler felt like a zit on a whore's ass. Two living humans in a river of mechatronics. That wasn't how he'd been trained to blend in.

As they neared the gate, an angular skull with three syringes sticking out of its cranium and an "x" over its mouth was painted on the wall. It was huge, probably three meters tall. Graffiti. On the wall and outside of it, no less. He'd never heard of something like that.

Two maintenance bots hovered near a display screen. Normally, the screen displayed instructions for human pilots coming into the gate, but now it was playing a video of LCP officers inside a residence tower. The video was from the perspective of one of the officers. It was distorted with noise, like old recordings—not a true syncast pattern—and it showed the officers chasing a group of kids up a stairwell, the camera bouncy and giddy. Tyler's mouth went dry, tasted like rot, when he realized what the video was from. The officers were shooting at the kids, high-fiving each other with every kill. The point of view pivoted to congratulate an officer behind him and Tyler could see further down the stairwell the men with the personal incinerators, saw the lightning flash of that contained inferno, saw the vacuum bots trundling behind.

"What is that," the boy whispered.

This was the sacrifice, a Culling, but not how it was supposed to be portrayed. Not awake. Solemn and sleeping under a syncast, not running. No high-fives. Certainly not reminding us there were children involved. The "In Memoriams" never mentioned the children. But they were there. Tyler knew they were there.

The video ended with a flicker and that same stylized skull with an "x" over its mouth on the screen, then looped and began again.

A security bot rolled towards them between the lanes of vehicles. It had a flat monitor for a head, two M243 miniguns mounted on either side of its body and it balanced on a pair of side-by-side wheels. It was scanning codes embedded in the doors of the vehicles, communicating with the pilot AIs, then moving along. When it reached Tyler's jeep it scanned the door, then blinked a series of colors at Tyler.

"No," Tyler said. "I have this." He held up the SLS ID badge and a red laser line scanned across it. The security bot blinked colors at Tyler again.

"No."

More colors.

"That's not—I have Cam-Tom clearance for this kid."

One final blink and the bot turned to leave.

"Dammit, no. I need—"

The jeep started moving on its own, the piloting system commandeered by Cerebus security.

"Shit," Tyler said. He checked that his Mark 37 was loaded with a round chambered.

"Remember," he said. "Move when I move."

They were guided into a service lane and stopped next to the main security office for the ground level. Inside, he could see several security officers. To his left, the stop-and-go traffic leaching through the gate. Tyler knew there would be gun turrets nestled in the ceiling. If it came to running, it would be hell, but maybe it wouldn't come to that. Maybe the SLS men hadn't been reported missing yet.

One of the officers approached. Tyler knew how they must look, the jeep crumpled and muddy, the kid in the orange jumpsuit, also muddy, covered in blood with a swollen cut over his eye. Why had he thought he could do this by himself?

Tyler held up the security badge. "I have Cam-Tom clearance. It's important I get through now." Calm. Authoritative.

The security guard noticed the JACKK arteries. "Oh," he said. "Ok. Um, hover tight a minute." He took Tyler's badge and returned to the station.

Movement in the rearview mirror grabbed Tyler's attention. An unmarked black van that practically screamed SLS creeped along the service lane and stopped at the end of the tunnel behind him, blocking their way back.

How in the hell? Of all the gates, of all the levels through the gate, how? Tyler opened his door and got out. He pulled on his backpack, buckled it across his chest, then slung on his Mark 37.

Six men in black uniforms with assault rifles climbed out of the van and started walking towards them. They moved tactically; slow and steady, spread out.

"Come here," Tyler said to the boy. The kid didn't move. Tyler leaned into the jeep and dragged him over.

At the other end of the tunnel ahead of him, another black van weaved against traffic until it was blocking the service lane. Again, six soldiers. None of them had raised their weapons. Yet.

One hundred fifty meters to get into Elia. There was no way to run and gun that far. Not with the kid. Not if he wanted the kid alive, at least. But maybe that was it? Everyone wanted the kid alive.

The security guard was returning now, trying not to look at the SLS men, but failing, then watching Tyler, probably hoping Tyler hadn't seen the approaching men yet. Tyler could smell the fear on him, could hear the short breaths. Maybe he was asking himself what Tyler had been wondering most of his life: why me?

"Please return to your vehicle," the guard said.

Tyler snapped open his MK-9's drop-leg holster.

"There's a mix up with your ID. It'll only take a minute." Tyler would have thought a High Laner could lie better than that.

The guard came around the front of the jeep, his left hand up. When he was within arm's reach, Tyler pulled his pistol and shot him between his eyes. The gunshot bellowed down the tunnel, declarative. Final. The boy screamed.

Before the SLS men could react, Tyler had the boy out of the jeep and the barrel of the MK-9 grinding against his temple.

The SLS men ran now, reached Tyler, formed a perimeter. Twelve of them, shoulder to shoulder, and he alone. Tyler envied their camaraderie, their backs covered, not threatened. A shared purpose. He envied their togetherness.

A siren cawed and red strobe lights spasmed across the tunnel walls. At each end of the passage, hatches slid open and two heavy gun turrets lowered, swiveling towards them, like starving bears wakened from hibernation.

"It'll never work," one of the men said.

Tyler wrapped his arm around the kid's neck. The boy was trembling.

"You know what I am," Tyler said. "You know I can kill this kid and seven of you before you even fire a shot." He walked backwards toward the end of the tunnel, the kid's feet barely touching the ground.

The SLS men kept pace; armed satellites waiting, waiting.

"He'll do it," the boy said. "Please help me."

"Shut up," Tyler said.

They had neared the end of the tunnel and Tyler was starting to feel like this could work when the crawlbot appeared. It looked like a crab, but instead of pincers were two railguns and its face was a cyclops-like sensor under an octagonal hood. The four-legged mech stepped over the SLS van and settled into position, bearing down on Tyler. The traffic was forced to stop.

"This is it," the SLS soldier said. "No further. We have two success conditions for our mission and neither of them require you leaving alive. Let the kid go." The guard's breath steamed between them, as if his threat had shape, lingered in the cold.

Tyler looked over his shoulder at the crawlbot and as he did so, spotted a small propane truck three lanes over. It was of the old style, with an exposed steel tank.

He reached behind him and pulled out one of his E15 incendiary grenades.

To the boy he said, "Cover your ears. This is going to hurt."

Using every bit of speed his JACKK would give him, Tyler armed the grenade, skated it under the cars towards the propane truck, holstered his MK-9 and dove on top of the kid.

The soldiers began shooting, careless if they hit the boy. Tyler felt the rounds smack into his melmoth vest, flattening out, the fibers rippling. One went through his right thigh, another through the vest into his side. Hot, ripping pain. His JACKK kicked into overdrive, smothering the pain. To Tyler's enhanced perception, it felt like he laid on that boy for an hour being shot, waiting, counting heartbeats until—

The grenade went off.

The concussion ripped apart the tank and the burning shrapnel ignited the fumes, turning the lower tunnel of Cerebus Gate North into Hell.

The things you think about at a time like this, flying through the air, gripping the child. Thinking how burning rubber and burning humans could smell so similar. The roar of the conflagration. The last time you were in a concrete building that exploded. Heat, searing and merciless. Hopeless. But you did hope, didn't you? Let this be the end. Let this erase your sins. But it didn't, did it? How could you think you would be let off that easy?

They hit the wall of the tunnel. Tyler couldn't quite hear yet, his nanocellotics still protecting his eardrums. He tried to leap to his feet, but the bullet in his thigh raged. He limped to the boy, scooped him up and shuffled to the end of the tunnel. Smoke swirled around them. The flames were searing Tyler's beard and face.

At the mouth of the tunnel, Tyler set the boy down as gently, but quickly as he could. Dead or unconscious? The crawlbot was trying to regain its footing, rocking back and forth to extricate its front leg from a logging truck that had rolled up on it. It spotted Tyler coming and opened up with its railgun, an angry chainsaw sound as thousands of superheated slugs exploded at mach seven from the rails, the bullets' metal casings melting and burning in gouts of flame. The rounds zipped over Tyler's head and decimated the wall behind him.

Tyler hobbled under the railgun, up the front leg and around the ammo box, to the pilot's hatch. The crawlbot bucked like a crazed bull. It took a full magazine and wild hopes of not being hit by a ricochet to puncture the latch. Crawlbot pilots had to lay on their stomach inside the mech using a combination of a synmap helmet and joysticks for navigation and weapons control. By the time Tyler had the hatch open, the pilot had rolled on his side, trying to get his sidearm aimed upwards, but pinning his elbow with his own body. They both shot at the same time. Only Tyler's rounds found their mark.

The smoke was starting to thin when Tyler got back to the boy. He was moving. Not dead, then. Tyler told himself the relief he felt was at knowing he could still finish his mission. Nothing more.

The nanocellotics were finally working and he was able to throw the kid over his shoulder like a sack and run, reloading his assault rifle with his other hand. The automated traffic coming through Cerebus had begun to move again, probably under commands to clear lanes for LCP security. He sprinted across the highway, stuttering screams from the semis' brakes as they tried to avoid him, and leapt over the concrete barrier to a culvert. He put down the kid, took cover behind the barrier and leveled his Mark 37 at the smoldering tunnel waiting for them. But, maybe there wouldn't be any "them." Nobody had been moving after the explosion. And if anyone did survive, they wouldn't know which way he went. Sit tight for a few seconds and then slip away.

Like ghosts, covered in concrete dust and fury, five SLS security soldiers limped out of the tunnel and stopped near the wrecked crawlbot. Four took defensive postures aiming in all directions while the fifth knelt and consulted some display on his rifle. After a

second, he peered across the highway. Through the traffic. At Tyler.

"The hell," Tyler said.

The five soldiers began moving towards them.

Up and running. For his life? How do you save a life that is already dead? Days from dead. Been dead for years. Carrying a life? Maybe, maybe not. A boy. But also a weapon. Just a little further. Just let him get a little further and then he'll figure it out. Tyler knew there was an "it" to figure.

Tired was something the syncasts made you feel after synthesizing you at a job, or helping you pretend you'd chased a criminal in an action story, or won a game of tackle splats. What Tyler felt, running from the SLS men, two bullets burrowing their way through his body with every bounce, was desperation. He'd checked the boy. Dammit, he'd checked. There were no cybernetics, no signs of implants. Was he in over his head? Was he alone enough to do what needed doing?

A bullet fizzled past his head, then the grunt of the shot followed. Pieces of the concrete culvert flicked up around his feet as more bullets landed close, but not quite.

They reached a metal ladder and Tyler slung the boy around his hip and used the other hand to scale the rungs, two at a time. Once out of the culvert they were in the Lower Skims. Plastic buildings with bloody rust-pocked steel doors pressed against each other like fake books on a shelf. Few people came out into the streets in the Skims. Why would they? What was there for them out here? Everything they needed was delivered to their door: nutrient sacs, synmap parts and syncasts, narcotics. It was the desperate — those who needed medical help or had overdrawn their narcs and nutrients or who were on a mandatory six hour relapse — it was desperation that drove those who ventured into the wild. But wasn't it always?

At the moment, Tyler wished there were more people on the streets. When he was a kid, he'd loved having the streets to himself while everyone else dreamed under the synmap. Now, he needed cover.

Down an alley between two residence towers. Dozens of ventilation fans spun in a hypnotizing pattern and conduit veined the buildings, crawling over gangways and service balconies. At the far end Tyler saw a garbage compactor. He ran to it and opened the hatch and told the boy to climb in. Maybe it would dampen whatever signal they were tracking the kid with. At the least it might slow a bullet. Desperate. But wasn't he always?

He watched from inside a ventilation shaft on the second floor above the kid's compactor. He'd torn out the grating and wedged his knife into the fan to stop the blade and slid into the tunnel, exposing just enough of himself to aim down the gangway toward the alley's entrance below. If they were coming, they'd be here any second.

Two grenades twirled into the alley, then exploded. The first was a flashbang. Tyler shut his flesh eye and turned his head and even so still watched the back of his eyelid go from red to pink to near white in an instant. The second spiraled, spewing some kind of gas.

The key to a soldier's strength and endurance is the efficient use of oxygen and thus was the first thing the Joint Autopharmaceutical and Cybernetics Kinesis Kit had to address. Tyler could hold his breath and function for upwards of nine minutes, fifteen if he was sitting still. This would be over in two.

The first four died quickly. Pop, pop. Pop, pop. Tyler had waited until all five were clear of the street, the first ones almost to the compactor, before he'd fired. They knew—thought they knew— that Tyler and the boy were in there. The fifth one, the one with whatever sensor they were tracking the kid with, fired back at Tyler before taking two rounds to the stomach. He grunted and sprawled backwards.

Tyler scrambled out of the tunnel.

The soldier was reaching for his rifle when Tyler stood on the gangway and fired twice more, blowing the man's arm apart. The soldier screamed.

Tyler pulled his knife out of the ventilation shaft and the fan began spinning along with the dozens of others. Already they had cleared the gas.

As he climbed down from the gangway, the kid was lowering himself out of the garbage compactor. Scarlet swelling from the gas rimmed his eyes. When he saw the soldier leaning against the wall, hugging his mutilated arm, a grisly blend of fabric and flesh smeared across the soldier's stomach, the kid whimpered and covered his face.

"How did you find us?" Tyler said.

"You have no idea," the soldier managed through clenched teeth.

"Let's go," the kid said, pulling on Tyler's sleeve.

"How are you tracking him?"

"He's not just a science experiment. They don't mobilize a crawlbot for nothing."

The man was right. A crawlbot. Military mech operating inside the Gates—technically illegal. And all for this kid. What was Tyler doing? He didn't even know how the kid worked or if he'd be able to activate whatever it was that the kid did? If he was going to make it the rest of the way through the city, he was going to need help. The city where Staern Life Sciences and the other Big Seven operated with impunity and the Liberty Conglomerate Province military could move on a moment's notice.

"Let him go, okay," the boy said. "Let him go and we can run. We can go now."

"Look at you," the soldier said. He had softened his voice despite the pain, as if to say, be reasonable. "Shot to hell. Barely able to stand. Even a JACKK can't take on the whole LCP military alone. Leave the kid and go. Maybe save yourself. Why do this? It's not worth it."

Worth. That was the word. To be worthy. When Tyler's watch ticked to zero, that word would be the difference.

The boy tugged again at Tyler's sleeve. "Let's go," he said. "Before more bad guys come."

"Bad guys?" Tyler looked at the boy. "Kid, that's all there are." He put his rifle to the soldier's forehead and fired once. After all, be reasonable.

The kid yelped, but didn't run. Already, then? A little less bothered by death?

There was a cable twisting from the soldier's rifle to a synport behind his right ear. Tyler picked up the rifle, then unplugged the jack from the dead soldier's head and connected it to his own synport. A spinning circle lit up in his vision as it synced with his Sakanaya. The monitor on the rifle blinked on and Tyler could see in his heads-up display, what was being shown on the monitor—a satellite view of the street with a blue dot labeled S04 and a red dot labeled C17 blinking behind him. Tyler turned to face the boy and as he did, the display reoriented itself, the red dot now in front of him. He walked up to the boy and the two dots touched.

The look on the boy's face. Fear? Guilt? Did he know this whole time?

"Where's the fucking bug?" Tyler whispered.

A MAN

Elia. Spanning what had once been fourteen different states and even parts of Canada now smudged together into a staccato city, citizens living near each other, but never knowing one another. Sharing space, sharing air, but nothing else. The wall loomed behind Tyler and the boy as they hustled through the Ottawa Ward. A city that spanned thousands of kilometers and still Tyler saw too much of himself everywhere. There the tower that Little Fit and Tyler had broken into for Tyler's first Ten-run with the Red Lithiums, there the tower that was Culled in '28. The relief they'd felt then, like a bolt of lightning so close they could feel the static charge, but death dodged. Soon they'd be near Liberty Heights. The place where he'd lived with his mother. Next to each other, but never knowing each other, not really. Not even at the end.

A burning afternoon sun colored the sign that said LCP Sanctioned Medical Provider. Painted over the words "medical provider" were the words "Meat Doctor."

"I can't..." the boy dropped to the concrete steps while they waited. Tyler let go of the boy's arm so he could lean against the railing. He'd been towing the boy along for five or six kilometers.

"They're going to come again," the boy said. He was breathing heavy. "They'll never stop."

"Whose fault is that?"

"My head hurts." Deciding what on the kid's face was dirt and what was blackening bruises was pointless. Part of his left eye looked misshapen because of the swelling around the cheek and a crust of blood rimmed the inside of his ears.

"That makes two of us," Tyler said. "Not much longer and it'll all be over."

Tyler could sense the green courage budding within the boy when the child said, "Those soldiers were people." He nodded, as if testing the idea. "Real people."

"So was I," Tyler said. He pressed the call button again. Looked at the security camera over the door. "So was my—"

A man from Eastern Eurasia with a wide nose opened the door and stood looking at Tyler, then at the boy, then back to Tyler and said, "I thought you'd be dead by now."

"There's something laced around his left ulna, but it's beyond anything I've ever seen." The boy was laying on a bio imager in the clinic. He was naked and they'd taken a couple minutes to clean him up as best they could. So he doesn't get my scanner dirty, the doctor had said.

Dr. Valadinar Makasihiro — Snip to his paying customers — the Red Lithiums. He wasn't very good at his job, but he was a cool cucumber when it came to blood and guts and gunshots. And he worked off the grid, so to speak, which made Lithium folks happy and had been key for Tyler after Liberty Heights.

"It's like a sleeve on the bone." The doctor handed Tyler a datapad. "It connects to his IV port at the fistula in his left elbow. Secondarily, there are millions of tiny packets lining his arteries. I thought they were a kind of malignancy at first, but imaging shows they are synthetic." He said it as sin-tetic.

Tyler rotated the view and zoomed in on one of the sacs.

"If you magnify enough, there is a protein strand connecting the fistula, the sleeve on the ulna and the sacs. Like a web or something. It seems the sleeve has both a receiver and transmitter built into it."

"Can you remove it?"

"Can you stop doing that please?" Tyler was tapping his MK-9 against his leg, a clicking sound as it hit his drop-leg holster.

"No," the doctor said.

"Can't or won't?"

"C'mon. This is the Lower Skims. My job is to give them a little extra portion of whatever narcs they need while letting them die. Even if I had the equipment for that kind of surgery, I wouldn't know where to start without taking the whole arm off."

"Okay. That."

"What? No. Stop." He put a hand to Tyler's chest. "I have no idea what will happen if you cut into that thing. You said he's a Cull? Whatever is inside him is how he executes his Culling. Those sacs are throughout his body."

The man was right. He'd end up killing himself and a stupid meat doctor for nothing. But that meant they were going to be tracking Tyler from here on. And that meant if he thought he was under a time crunch before…

"Is that thing right? Three and a half days?" The doctor was looking at Tyler's watch. "You look like shit. Are you feeling any Denoument Effects?"

"I need a fast way into the Veil. And don't say the Red Lithiums." Then, to the kid, "Get up and get dressed." The doctor had found new clothes for the boy, a t-shirt with the LCP President's seal on the front and the words "Together in Hope."

Tyler began stripping out of his bloody and burned SLS uniform.

"They're the only way," the doctor said. He handed Tyler the pants out of his backpack.

"Not an option. What about this new group? A skull and syringes coming out of its head. I saw it outside the Gate."

"The Silent Uprising? Stay away from them. If there's a public enemy number one, they're it."

"That might be alright. I'm looking to take over that spot myself."

The doctor was holding Tyler's shirt, but didn't hand it to him. Tyler snapped his fingers to get the doctor to focus, then took the shirt.

"They're some kind of revolution, protesting the Cullings and the Resource Gap. Definitely a mix of High Laners and Skimmers and they're able to move between the Veil, it seems, but either way, the only way I can think of to reach them would be the Red Lithiums."

Tyler finished buckling his drop-leg rig together and shoved the MK-9 into its holster. He took the backpack from the doctor.

"I'll be damned if I ever go back to those snakes. Still letting the Lithiums kick you in the nuts?"

"Is stopping an option?"

Tyler finished pulling the backpack on and then guided the kid to the door. "Same deal as last time," Tyler said. "Mute on me being here and you have nothing to fear."

"Don't worry," the doctor said. "I have a feeling this really is the last time I'll see you alive."

The sound the trains made as they flurried in, stopped and settled on their rails, was not unlike a sigh, a release of tension. Tyler and the boy hid in an alley, clear firing lanes ahead, no ambush threats behind. He'd pulled over a Trash Zapper just large enough for the boy to squeeze behind and Tyler had covered himself and his weapons with his thermal blanket. It didn't take much for him to look dead or, at the least, like someone else's problem. Grey clad LCP employees alighted from the train, typing on the sleeves of their jackets, subconsciously weaving like salmon around those heading home for the evening. Tyler had the feeling they were weaving into a net. Out of a net? They were the only ones who had authorization—dared—to travel by train through the Veil between the High Lanes and the Lower Skims.

Look at those 'netics, Tyler thought. He could barely see the seams where flesh touched silicone. If he'd thought his Sakanaya metal was the cat's meow, it was clear they'd held back on the best. Figures. One more middle finger he'd gotten in this life. Nothing but the best, for the best, they'd said. God, Tyler was sick of being lied to.

How to get on that train? "Me and this boy are on our way into town to kill one of the Big Seven CEOs" probably wouldn't cut it. What, then? How does the Devil sneak into Heaven?

A solid-food vendor rumbled up to the train's platform on his motorized kitchen, cubes of cupboards and ovens stacked and bolted together, a marvel of gyroscopes and balance on two wheels. Smoked meats and sausages swung on strings from the awning and small fans spread smells that sawed at Tyler's stomach. That venison was the last thing he'd eaten. Since then he'd been in a hell of a fight and his JACKK had devoured everything he had to keep him alive.

"I'm hungry," the kid said.

The Silent Uprising? Were they the only way in? Tyler had never heard of a revolution before, had never imagined the possibility. No

Skimmer would dare revolt. Why should they? And the idea that High Laners could bring themselves to care about Skimmers…Tyler felt ridiculous even thinking it. But maybe? And if so, that meant they moved through the Veil.

Reaching them, though, was the real problem. Connections. In a world where Skimmers live and die without ever seeing the person in the cubit next to them, how do you find someone who knows someone who knows about a revolution? And fast. Even now the kid was sending signals that someone somewhere was tracking. He had hours, maybe minutes.

A man with dark skin and a grey beard, wearing a vinyl coat without a shirt underneath ambled up the stairs onto the train platform. Rusted cables hung from the man's synports like Medusa's snakes. The solids vendor waved the man away before he'd even reached the top of the platform, then shoved him when he didn't stop. The man lost his balance and fell backwards, not trying or not able to stop himself.

"What's wrong with him?" the boy asked.

"He's cold-hacked. Happens if you refuse to come up for mandatory relapses."

Tyler could feel the reality of the situation settling around him like concrete. Heavy and immovable. Snip was right. He had no choice. Could one option be called a choice? Once again with having no choices. The Red Lithiums. It had been eight years. Maybe they wouldn't recognize him? He knew he looked different now, the JACKK swelling him, filling his chest and arms with murder. Either way, this time would be different.

The cold-hacked man sat looking at the cart. Then, while the solids vendor was helping a young High Laner woman, he stood up and tried to pull a swinging sausage. It didn't come loose, instead tipping the cart off balance. The gyroscopes whined to stabilize and the vendor dropped the box of pickled mushrooms and olives he'd mixed for the woman and wedged himself under the cart to keep it from falling.

"Oh no," the boy said.

The man stopped pulling at the sausage and started to back away, but too late. The vendor came at him and hammered his fist into the man's chin, then, when the man was on the ground, landed two kicks to his stomach and one to his face.

"Stop him," the boy said, looking at Tyler.

The vendor crouched over the man and said something Tyler couldn't hear. The High Laner woman walked away.

"Let's go," Tyler said.

"Why doesn't anybody help him?"

The cold-hacked man huddled against the gate at the top of the stairs.

Tyler had almost finished folding up his thermal blanket when he realized the boy was running across the platform. He started to chase the kid, but stopped when he felt his sidearm bounce against his thigh. He couldn't be seen like this. He retreated back into the alley, fury thrumming through him.

When the boy spoke to the vendor, it was as if they were old friends, remembering each other, laughing at a shared history, and then the vendor pulled down a sausage and gave it to the boy. They hugged. The boy jogged to the cold-hacked man still huddled on the ground, broke off part of the sausage and gave the man the larger piece. Something was said between them that pained the boy as he ran back to Tyler.

The kid took a bite of the sausage, the salty, smoky smells from the vendor sticking to him. He didn't look at Tyler while he chewed.

Seconds passed before Tyler was calm enough to speak. "Why?"

"He was hungry."

"How did you convince him?"

"I asked. People do things when I ask. You should try."

Tyler hauled the kid down the alley by the collar. He looked behind them as they walked away, down the alley to the sunlit platform. The cold-hacked man chewed slowly, almost not chewing at all, as if the meat were a sucker to be savored, his eyes closed.

"Pointless," Tyler said. "You know that, right? He's still going to die and nobody anywhere ever will give a shit."

The kid fought out from Tyler's grip.

"I do."

By the time they had made their way out of the Ottawa Ward and into Red Lithium territory, night had settled. And still no further pursuit from Staern. Tyler didn't know what to make of that. Part of him suspected they were trying to figure out why a JACKK would be involved in this and how to retrieve the kid before Tyler could react or kill him. Another part worried they were biding time. Time, the one thing Tyler couldn't beat.

Elia was a dark city. An upside down abyss where the stars in the sky took on the look of hope and warmth while the windows of the world were inky caverns, hiding sleeping inhabitants. Dreaming. Living polymer lives, seamed and crafted.

Tyler hadn't spent much of his life under the synmaps like everyone else. Illusions held little for him. Now, crossing this city, coming home, to a second home he'd fled, he had to wonder if a life of real suffering had at all been better than one of synthetic pleasures.

Blood soaked Tyler's belt and waistband. The injuries in his side and leg had yet to regurgitate the bullets and close, almost twenty-four hours after the fight at Cerebus Gate, as sure a sign of his impending death and the failure of his nanocellotics as any.

He'd had to carry the kid the last couple of hours through Elia, exhaustion ruining him. At first he'd begrudged the burden, but then there'd been something disturbingly comforting about the child's head resting on Tyler's shoulder, the boy's warm breath on his neck. Now the boy was awake, his head swiveling, tense.

The elevator clawed its way skyward, seeking the forty-fourth floor of a residence tower. Inside, Tyler and Ben stared at the closed doors. A massive pill had been stenciled on them, half red, half black, so that when the doors closed they formed a full pill.

"Where are we going?" the kid asked.

"To see some old friends," Tyler said. He could see his reflection in the chrome doors; squared head and neck that sloped into a bear's shoulders. He looked nothing like he did eight years ago. And even if they did recognize him, he was nowhere near as weak. It wouldn't be like last time. So why the fear?

After a minute, the boy said, "I thought all your friends tried to kill you."

**

The forty-fourth floor of the residence tower was rotting. Carpeting was torn and missing, zig zag strips of glue glaring like tears in a worn skirt. The doors to the rooms were off their rails and inside people laid on floors or slumped against walls while plugged into synmaps. Small fires burned in ceramic bowls. Ceiling tiles were missing and cables hung like vines. But it was the smell that told Tyler he had found the right tower.

The boy gripped Tyler's sleeve and said, "I want to go back."

At the end of the hallway, they walked onto a balcony. There, sprawled between this tower and the next was a fort of suspended shipping containers and tarps, a colony built against gravity, hidden under a skypass highway. The wind screeched, intense and constant, harmonizing with the traffic overhead. The boy gasped when he saw how high up they were.

Big S1m was a psycho, but a psycho with a vision, Tyler would give him that. In a world where the government rules every waking minute, literally telling you when to sleep and when to wake, who stands on a street corner, looks up and says, there, that empty space between those two buildings right there, that's the place I'll build my empire? Yet, that's exactly what the man had done. A cobweb of containers, flatbed trailers and rope ladders. A nest for the ones who didn't want to go to bed when Big Brother said it was time to sleep. For years, it had been Tyler's nest. Until they'd kicked him out, at least.

Tyler'd never learned the whole story of how Big S1m built his empire — and an empire it was—but it had started very much like Tyler's own. Awake on relapse, parent (parents?) back under, not giving too many shits if their son plugged in on time or not, and out of the house. Well, cubit. They didn't have houses in the Lower Skims. Those were in the syncasts. Anyway, maybe S1m runs into another kid up and about. Maybe they spot one of those Hamatino drones zipping through the hall delivering narc sacs and he decides to snag one. This is a capital offense, of course, the kind of thing that gets you a special narc sac all your own that you don't ever relapse from. These two kids, on second thought, maybe not kids, old enough to know something about the world, so let's say twelve or thirteen, they take these narc sacs to a train depot like the one Tyler was at earlier today — and this is the part where you see just how big those steel balls of S1m's are—he walks up to the first High Laner he sees and he offers to sell the sac for a bite of real food. Two capital offenses, but whose counting, right? Can't kill you twice. Somehow, in the dice rolls of dice rolls, Big S1m, had found the one fucking tweaker coming off that train that day. Tyler wondered if that High Laner was still alive and if he knew he'd started what would go on to be the only known human encampment outside of the High Lanes where people actually lived next to each other, awake, making conversation? Where the only body they ever had was the one they were in. The only encampment where men lived as men.

"Stay close," Tyler said to the boy. "Don't look at, touch or speak to anyone. These people will eat you. Got it?"

The kid nodded. There was white all the way around his eyes. He maybe thought Tyler meant they would literally eat him. If so, good. Terror was the only appropriate emotion for these people.

Climbing with the boy on his back, Tyler could feel the bullets chewing away inside him. He was stopped at the first level by three guards. The leader had a skin-mocked throat, the muscles and tendons made visible through translucent skin, so that as he demanded Tyler hand over his weapons, Tyler could see those muscles stretch and pull. He didn't recognize the other two, but the skin-mocked thug looked familiar. As he dredged for the man's name, a part of him understood the thug might be doing the same with Tyler, trying to remember the last time he'd seen him, remembering the last time he'd tried to kill this stranger.

A few seconds later the name came to Tyler. Crupps. The dumb fucking names. That was one thing Tyler was glad to be rid of when he'd left (ran for his fucking life, truth be told). They'd even given Tyler his own stupid name: Squeak. So, Crupps was the muscle now? Got a skin job on his throat and wanted to be a tough guy?

Crupps had been there the day they'd ganked him. He'd only kicked Tyler once he was down, though. The memories blended a slurp of anger and terror behind Tyler's eyes.

Five years he'd spent with them. Five years running some of the

best gap-rackets ever run, making all of them rich and free. And together. Then one day it was "together, but without you." In fact, without you alive at all. Well, you'd tried motherfuckers. You'd tried and failed and I wasn't even JACKK'd yet, Tyler thought. That was eight years ago and Tyler'd be lying if he said he was over it. He'd also be lying if he said he wasn't still a little afraid of Big S1m.

"In your dreams," Tyler said when Crupps reached for his rifle.

"You ain't LCP up here," Crupps said. "Big S1m says no guns in his presents." The "t" was distinct. Muscle, not brains.

"I'm the present," Tyler said, but he didn't move to offer his guns.

Crupps shrugged. "See how well you and the boy fly, then, when he throws you off."

Four more levels and they were to Big S1m. God, Tyler hated that name, too. He'd always called the guy B.S. The double meaning hadn't been lost on Big S1m.

As they approached Big S1m's container, four barefooted children buzzed between them, playing a game of chase. They lured the kid's attention, his head swiveling to follow the fun, and Tyler had to yank his arm to keep him close.

Dread sluiced through Tyler as they opened Big S1m's shipping container. He could still feel the man's hand on his shoulder that day. "Big run for a big man," he'd said as he'd sent Tyler on that last delivery to Cerebus. A father sending his son to do a man's work. They hadn't waited more than a block or two before they'd started in on Tyler.

His first thought when the door opened was Big S1m had gained weight. He sat in a wooden chair — wood!—with a little girl on his lap which looked more like a table of purple veined flesh than legs. His left leg had been removed below the knee, a cybernetic foot shaped like a clydesdale's hoof in its place and he'd replaced his lower jaw since Tyler saw him last. The new one was steel with jagged teeth like a bear trap and it was discolored where drool glistened on the edges. A DANGER sticker along the chin. He and the girl were plugged into a holodeck, controlling two robots fighting each other. Next to him sat a dark-haired woman. Evee. Her name came easier. Evee Malters. So she'd made her way to Big S1m himself. Tyler wasn't surprised. She'd probably humped her way up the food chain. Not surprised, but more frightened than before. She'd always been one for faces and names. His heart clawed at the inside of his ribs when her eyes lasered over him.

Big S1m unplugged the holodeck from his synport, then pushed the girl off of his legs. A cup of Nihonshu slopped when she kicked the table in front of them while climbing onto Evee's lap.

Humming wind and traffic filled the silence while Big S1m and Tyler stared at each other. Evee hunted Tyler's face, squinted. He could hear the kids' playing feet drumming against the deck outside. Crupps stood behind him, the second and third guards, further back at the door.

"You let him keep his thumpers?" Big S1m said. He never took his eyes off of Tyler's. "Nobody brings thumpers around my girls."

The metal chompers hadn't helped B.S.'s grammar any.

Crupps poked Tyler in the back and whispered, "Told you. Better grow some wings, flyboy."

"I just need to talk."

"Maybe I toss my crap-ass security, too."

Tyler watched as Crupp's naked throat muscles swallowed.

"How do I reach the Silent Uprising?" Tyler remembered how much Big S1m liked to talk. Nobody had time for that shit. Or for those rusted gears Evee called a brain to click into place.

Big S1m dabbed a cloth at the drool on his steel jaw. "He's direct, at least," he said. "That blood or piss?"

Everyone started to laugh and Tyler looked down to see his crotch soaked with blood from the bullet in his side. Crupps screeched his laugh, a dying rabbit sound, and Tyler noticed Evee shoot Crupps a disgusted look. Not on the food chain, then, it appeared.

"I heard a Twitcher banged up Cerebus Nort' this morning."

"Twitcher and a boy," Crupps said.

"Somes of us wondered what a JACKK does fighting into the Lower Skims and not out. Somes of us wondered why he fights his boss-folk."

"I just need to talk to them," Tyler said. "And the boy didn't bang up anything."

"Nah, the boy is for the banging, right?" Crupps humped the air with his hips. What would the man's neck muscles look like under Tyler's fingers?

"What's banging mean?" the boy asked.

"Ping the Silent Uprising for me. That's all I'm asking."

"Don't know 'em."

"Don't want to know those flag fappers." Crupps made a stroking gesture.

"Frag that. Lower Skims got noise you ain't hearing? And I saw their mark all over Cerebus."

"What if they not interested in talking to you? Hmm? They's got their own wars to wage, for some rabid-bitch reason."

Big S1m didn't build this empire on balls of steel alone. Considering him anything close to stupid had gotten more men launched forty stories to splat than Tyler cared to remember. The things that happened to a body hitting the ground at or near terminal velocity…it was the stuff of the really dark syncasts. Tyler had seen it enough times to know his kit wouldn't do boo with something like that. So when Big S1m said "what if they not interested," Tyler couldn't help but think the man was hiding something. That the question he was asking wasn't the question he wanted answered. And in that case, it was usually best not to answer at all.

"A JACKK and them's crusaders holding hands," Big S1m said when it was clear Tyler wasn't talking. "They headaches enough. Might be worth a lot to keeps you twos from talking."

"Mr. Tyler, what's banging mean?" The boy tugged at Tyler's pouches.

Evee was back to Sherlocking Tyler's face. He needed to wrap this up fast.

Tyler pulled out Eddie Fahrs's credit chip.

"Thirty-thousand," he said.

"Maybe chips don't interest me."

"Maybe chips don't interest him," Crupps said.

"Get off it. We both know you'd sell your own daughter." Or a a son.

Big S1m stabbed a finger at Tyler. "That be a hell of a thing to say to someone you's just met. Maybe I take the chips and toss you's out of my home. How be Twitchers at flying?"

Behind Tyler, Crupps was pulling back his coat. Tyler could hear the drag of the nylon over a metal gun grip. Evee tried not to look at the movement, tried not to reveal the ambush, but it was too late.

Then it occurred to Tyler: if he were making a list of people who'd fucked him in this life, the pole position went to Staerns, that's solid, but that number two slot? Tyler was in a room filled with them. Sure, a couple innocents, too, but don't kid yourself. Nobody is ever truly innocent. After all, wasn't Tyler the present?

"I don't relish the idea of killing everyone in here," Tyler said, "but if that bit-monkey behind me moves another centimeter I will lose it and all of this—" Tyler waved at Big S1m's wife and daughter, "—all this family shit you're playing at will come tumbling down with us. All I want is a meet and greet. Ping the Silent Uprising. That's it. Thirty-k richer."

Tyler could sense the boy's attention swing from the kids playing outside to Tyler. A studied fear searching for the bluff in his words.

"Maybe not so wise of a Twitcher, eh? Talking like that."

Big S1m clacked his metal teeth together. The DANGER sticker glistened.

"Thirty for a ping. Sure. Turns out, they want to meet you, too. Already called in case you showed up. Offering chips for a talk. And the boy. Good chips on meeting the boy." Big S1m settled back into his seat, signaling Crupps to settle as well. "But I do wonder what a Twitcher does killing LCP and talking to crusaders?" He dabbed again at the drool on his jaw. "I teach mine not to bite the hand that feeds them."

"Kid," Tyler said, "banging is what happens to suckers. I've learned that while one hand is feeding you, the other is probably pulling a knife to slit your throat."

Outside of B.S.'s container, Tyler waited for the Red Lithiums to make contact with the Silent Uprising and coordinate a meeting. The skin-mocked soldier and three others stood guard by him. He watched the boy running with the other children, leaping over small crates, climbing the nets. They had accepted him into their play group without hesitation, someone new, with new ideas for the

game, new tactics they'd never tested. Nothing demanded. No tests
of loyalty or schemes of what they could convince this new child to
do. The only requirement was that he play to win.

This was how man was built, Tyler thought. This is what had
sucked Tyler into the Red Lithiums. Yes, you had to accept murder
with the love, but didn't everyone? Didn't the High Laners accept
the murder of the Lower Skimmers in exchange for the connection
and love of their own families? But the Lower Skimmers didn't
murder and they didn't love. They didn't connect. Electrodes in
their brain mimicked connections, but the lives they touched and
that touched them were only buffered bits. Data. Simulated selves.

The boy ran up to Tyler, breathless, burning cheeks from the
Autumn air. Already the cut on his forehead looked better, the
bruising yellowing and fading. He wasn't moving like he was in an
explosion several hours ago.

"We should stay here." Stated. As if it were that simple.

"What?"

"With your friends. And I could play. And they could help you
not die."

Like a car rolling down a hill, his reaction caught itself up in its
own cascading gravity and Tyler knew it was too much, but didn't
want to stop himself. This was how they'd gotten him last time, this
facade of family that hid real betrayal.

He jerked the boy by the arm, smashing his nose into the child's.
"Listen, you little shit. They're not my friends. And they're not
yours. They'll sell you outside the LCP to a rape farm in a second.
Be grateful I'm here to protect you. We are leaving. Get ready."

The boy's eyelids had slackened into a resigned gaze while Tyler
was yelling. He wasn't afraid. All of that anger for nothing. If
anything, Tyler thought the boy offered a look of pity.

The other kids had stopped running and were watching them.
The wind moaned through the suspended base.

"Not everyone hates everyone else, wants to be alone all the
time," the boy said. "Just you."

It was possible to imagine everyone in the Lower Skims were
dead, an apocalypse erasing all life, that's how empty the streets

were. Big S1m, the skin-mocked soldier, Tyler and the boy rode in the back of B.S.'s Mananz MRS, facing each other.

"They said, 'No time like the present,'" Big S1m said. "But seemed to Big S1m they maybe hiding their antsy."

They'd given Tyler his weapons back, so why did he feel so vulnerable right now? He had to keep pushing the kid away from him, keeping space to move should he need.

"Especially the boy. They said, 'No deal without the boy.' Your mama in the crusades?"

Behind them, Tyler watched the two black motorcycles of the rear escort, their two riders each covered head to toe in black armor, like bulbous shadows. He knew there were another two in front.

"Didn't talk like a bunch of gomps who spray paint skulls, none neither," Big S1m said. "No noise. Just meet and time and place. Crispy." He wiped at his jaw with a cloth, waiting for Tyler to say something.

The boy had bunched the bottom hem of his "Together in Hope" t-shirt into a ball and was twisting it.

"Don't operate like gomps neither. Make Red Lit biz harder, more expensive. Crusaders always blowing up LCP trucks and trains, spreading their syncast noise. Big bosses start cracking down on Skimmers leaving their holes, shorter relapses. And for what? Skimmers don't care none. They's none care. Hundred years things be what they be with resource gap and all and now some crusaders cracking the boat."

"Rocking the boat," Tyler said.

They sloped downward into a tunnel and the inside of the car darkened, the signal lights coloring everything amber. Big S1m was searching Tyler's face, seeking any answers he might divine there, like casted bones. For a man used to being the center of everyone's interest, the catalyst, Tyler knew Big S1m must hate this diminishing ignorance.

"You familiar to me," Big S1m said.

Tyler felt his heart drop, as if it dragged along the pavement beneath the car.

"You have a brother?"

"Maybe their minds changed," Big S1m said.

They had parked at Enimel Industries's wharf in the Eleventh district. Several warehouses and an office building ringed the outside perimeter and no ships were moored to the quays. Big S1m's soldiers leaned against their motorcycles yapping, wagging their hands as they made jokes with each other. Tyler was annoyed at their complete lack of readiness.

Ben was rubbing at his left arm, above the IV port. He said, "My arm hurts."

Tyler heard the craft approaching up the Little Marek river long before the others did. Once it was in range, they could see it was a small insertion craft with a forward mounted 20mm autocannon and five men on board. It was LCP military gear.

Tyler loosened his Mark 37 off of his shoulder and moved next to the boy who was still massaging his arm. "Stay close," he said.

"It really hurts," the boy said.

The boat glided up against the quay and a magnetic clamp snapped out and reeled the craft in. A ramp automatically extended out from the ship and four soldiers and a woman disembarked. The soldiers moved well, their weapons ready, but not raised. They wore helmets that covered their eyes and their noses and mouths were covered by nylon masks. A white skull with an "x" over the mouth was painted on each. Synmap cables looped from their helmets like braids.

The woman was meaty, middle aged, with grey stains in her brown hair. For some reason the grey hair reminded Tyler that growing old was something he would never do. She had a granite face with a straight line for a mouth.

They stopped some distance from Big S1m and the Red Lithiums.

"Incredible." The woman was looking at the boy.

"What's not incredible is that we bring them to you," said Big S1m, louder than he needed to. Nervousness? Tyler couldn't believe it, but maybe? "On time. What is incredible is that you think we turn over the boy and the man for so little."

"This is," the woman took a deep breath and held it, then let it out slowly, "frustrating."

The Red Lithium soldiers weren't leaning on their motorcycles anymore. Tyler eased the boy behind him.

"LCP pays big bucko's for rogue Twitcher and little boy," Big S1m said.

"You don't..." The woman laughed and looked at the Silent Uprising soldier next to her, then back at Big S1m. "You don't even know who the buyer would be. Liberty isn't looking for them. Staern Life Sciences are."

"Same shit. Different asshole."

"No," she said, her voice like embers. "They're not."

Tyler wanted to scream. How could he be so stupid? How could he have thought that this once, just this once, Big S1m would actually do what he said he would do? He flicked off the safety on his rifle.

"My stomach hurts," the boy said to Tyler. He was holding his belly now.

"Your people are already taking delivery," the soldier next to the woman said to Big S1m.

"You've had that treehouse for what? Fifteen, sixteen years," the woman said. "And the police never bothered to look up in all that time? Never wondered what that mess of cables and plastic was up there?"

"Not very curious, those ones," Big S1m said.

"You should go home," the woman said. Tyler was impressed with her composure, the way she clipped each word with finality, but never hurried, not a whiff of fear. "Bundle up your wives and kids. They're important to you people, right? I'm worried the LCP has gotten inquisitive. And in case you think I'm not being fair, you can keep the Twitcher."

"No dice," Tyler said. "Package deal, lady. And you," he turned to Big S1m, "You always were full of BS. But you know the difference between us? I'm not. I swear to you on my left fucking nut, I will use my final hours on this earth to ravage everything you hold dear in life and then I will end that life. That goes for both of you." He turned back to the woman. "This is a simple swap. Keep it that way."

Big S1m was squinting at Tyler, working his metal jaw back

and forth. "Squeak?" he said to Tyler. "That you? You go and get JACKK'd?"

"Please, Mr. S1m," the boy said in a pinched voice. He was still holding his sides. "He'll do it. He kills everyone. He—" The boy screamed, then buckled forward, landing hard on his knees and kicking his legs out. He lay thrashing on the concrete wailing.

"The fuck—" Big S1m started to say.

Tyler moved first, of course. He stepped next to Big S1m and slammed his rifle's barrel up against the man's prosthetic jaw, the clink of metal on metal. "It won't hurt going in, but it'll probably hurt coming out," Tyler said.

Behind Big S1m, Tyler watched as the air folded in on itself, warping like a mirror starting to melt, then swept backwards to reveal four more Silent Uprising soldiers in flanking positions behind the Red Lithiums. Adaptive camouflage. This wasn't kid stuff. Whoever was funding the Silent Uprising had connections. This gave Tyler hope they would actually be able to get him through the Veil after all. If they didn't all die here first.

Another Silent Uprising soldier ran up to the boy and put handcuffs on him.

"He might explode," the woman said. "We're leaving."

The soldier cradled the boy in his arms and began walking to the boat while the other Silent Uprising soldiers backpedaled slow and steady, their weapons never leaving their targets.

"Explode?" Big S1m said.

Tyler followed their lead and backed up to the boat as well. At the edge of the wharf, he turned to get on, but a soldier stopped him and held up a pair of manacles. They were larger than handcuffs, designed for a Twitcher's strength.

"Piss off," Tyler said.

"It's the only way you're getting on this boat," the woman said.

He needed her more than she needed him and they both knew it. If he still wanted to get through the Veil, this was his way. He handed his rifle to the soldier and then cuffed himself. The soldier leaned out of the boat and took Tyler's MK-9 out of his hip holster.

As Tyler climbed into the boat, Big S1m called out to him. "Hey Squeak." Tyler turned. "Once a sucker, always a sucker."

Water sprayed across the bow, crystal globs catching the moonlight. The boat's engines were silent, so all Tyler heard was the slap of the water on the hull and the buzz of drones. One of the Silent Uprising soldiers knelt next to the boy who was laying on the deck and plugged a monitor with a long tube into the port in his left arm. The boy had stopped spasming and was now whimpering while he held his stomach. The man had to force his arm open to reach the port.

"Get away from him," Tyler yelled.

The man ignored him, looking instead at the display connected to the boy's IV.

Tyler hated being handcuffed, feeling weak. He put his boot to the man's shoulder and shoved hard. The man crashed into the side of the craft.

"Please stop," the woman said.

The man righted himself and said to the woman, "It's not the steg. We're okay."

She nodded, then to Tyler, "He's not hurting him. He's echoing the signal SLS is using to track the boy so we can mask it."

"What's happening to him?"

"They're endeavoring to slow him—and you — down. Probably preparing a larger assault team to eliminate you and recover him. That Malcolm Staern." She smiled as she said this.

Water was pooling around the boy's face, but he didn't seem to notice. Tyler eased his foot under the kid's head like a pillow.

Power was a real thing in a vague word. It was the thing Tyler had at one time and wanted back, the thing he had spent most of his short adult life taking. He knew this. Some people didn't know why they did what they did, but not Tyler. He knew.

So when they arrived in a warehouse, the bay doors dropping like jaws into the canal, and Tyler saw the men with the set-up they were assembling, he knew his power had been stolen.

One of the soldiers with the white "x" painted over his mask carried the boy across the warehouse towards a stainless steel table on wheels. It had been rolled over a clear tarp, the plastic bunched up around the wheels like snow drifts. Two men in green smocks hovered over a utility cart setting out tools: a reciprocating saw, scalpels, and a long glass canister with a steel base and tubes inside of it. Its hatch was open, waiting.

The soldier laid the boy on the table.

Tyler tested the handcuffs. He wouldn't be able to break them.

"I'm going to need that boy back," he called.

The rest of the Silent Uprising soldiers had disembarked and the woman smiled at Tyler, then offered her hand to help him up. He didn't take it.

"Let's talk." She waved at one of the soldiers and he set out two metal stools several meters from the table with the boy. She sat like a man, hunched forward with her legs spread, intense, though Tyler noticed, even spread, her thighs still touched. A High Laner who loved and could afford solid foods, then. You don't get thighs like that on nutrient sacs.

"You seem like you'd have a fascinating story," she said.

"I don't have time for stories. I need to get into the Veil."

"Humor me. How did you find the boy?"

Tyler tried, as slowly as possible, to pull on the handcuffs to test them again. Six centimeters between his wrists and they'd left his hands in front of him. That gave him options. He counted soldiers in the warehouse. Sixteen. That limited his options.

"He found me," Tyler said. "Old man and him were stealing my shit."

"Outside the wall? Why'd you come through Cerebus like that?"

Six soldiers next to them. Two behind Tyler, four around the woman. They carried Jackson & Sons 7Ms, close-quarters alternates to Tyler's Mark 37. Military grade shit.

"In Wisconsin."

"Wisconsin." She was good at controlling her expressions, Tyler noticed, that half smile never flagging under her surprise. "What were you doing on the edge of LCP territory?"

The kid moaned and rolled over so that one leg was dangling off of the table. One of the men in the green smocks grabbed it and hauled the kid back up. Tyler didn't like how rough the man was about it.

"I'd been there a couple years. Listen, is he going to be ok? I need him. If he's not going to be, I need to get moving."

"We don't have a lot of time, no. That's why I need to understand first. Help me. My name is Sara Lemira."

Names were power. He didn't want to reveal his, but what choice did he have? He never had any fucking choices.

"Tyler."

"Tyler, do you know what that boy is?"

"I know all about him." There was a line to what Tyler would admit. Ignorance was on the other side of it.

"Then, you know who made him and what he does?"

"Yup."

The kid screamed, stomping his heels against the table.

Sara smiled and ran a hand through her hair. Silver and brown strands twisted between her fingers. "What I'm trying to decide, Tyler, is if we can help each other, because if we can, I think we could do something great together, but if we can't, I need to make some fast decisions on what to do with you and that boy. Lying to me isn't helping."

She was right and Tyler knew it.

"He's a Cull," Tyler said. "Staern Life Sciences designed him to be…" What had Glasses said? "…a less invasive Cull."

"So you know how he works? Why do you need to get through the Veil? Are you, Tyler, taking him back?"

"Yeah."

"We know you're not working for SLS or the LCP military…"

"I'm going to find Malcolm Staern and I'm going to blow us all to Hell."

"Us."

"Staern, the kid and me." Tyler tapped his watch. "Time's running out."

That seemed to be what Sara wanted to hear, her play-it-cool mask giving a little too much away.

"So you plan to use the overclock?"

Tyler had never in his life had a play-it-cool mask, so he wasn't surprised when she spotted his confusion like spotting a hair on a whore's tit.

"That's what I thought. Couple years in Wisconsin, you said? Ok, here's the short version."

Turned out Tyler had thrown more shit at the fan than he ever realized two years ago in Liberty Heights. This Sara chick started talking about a residence tower and how it came crashing down during the last Culling. She asked Tyler if he had heard about it or seen it and Tyler had to keep himself from scoffing—barely able to nod. Seen it? Sure. Heard about it? More like his nanocellotics did everything they could to mute the sound as it crashed around him. Anyway, this kicks a hornets' nest nobody, not Sara, not Staern, not President Thatcher of the LCP, definitely not Tyler, knew existed. Something about that building coming down, the carelessness of it all, rattled people's cages. As if the country just then realized there were people in that building. Dead was dead. Tyler didn't get it. They hadn't had a problem sending cops in with personal-incinerators and vacuum bots, but for the love of God, a building comes down and now we understand that people were dying? The fuckers.

People in the High Lanes started speaking out. Not necessarily everywhere, but at home, to each other, around the dinner table. Tyler could see it like in the syncasts he'd play through as a child. Honey glazed salmon on the end of their fork, bobbing between them as if on waves of indignation as they started to say things like, "This is horrifying. Somebody should do something."

Sara Lemira happened to be one of those people, but she'd "never been one to wait for someone to hitch her pony for her" so she decided she should be the someone doing something. Enough people were squawking that when she and a couple like-minded fella's started feeding syncasts into the system revealing what actually happened during Cullings, those squawks turned into screams. High Laners weren't fans of LCP's propaganda lies— that this wasn't a peaceful, sacred affair, but a simple slaughter of innocents.

"And then the Kibashi girl happened," Sara said.

"Kibashi Communications?"

"The same. The only child of Himoto Kibashi. She walks up to their headquarters in Central Fields, head shaved, dressed like a Skimmer with a synmap plugged in and she sets herself on fire. Right there. The assumed heir burns to death in front of her dad's company in protest of the Cullings."

"She killed herself," Tyler said. "For Skimmers?"

"Unreal, right? Something had to be done."

"Lady, this is fascinating, but…" Tyler tapped his watch again.

"The boy, Tyler. He's the something. Malcolm Staern," Sara smiled. "The man's a genius. He knew if he could declare—or tell the LCP president to declare—that Cullings were being ended, that would remove the raison d'être for the Silent Uprising. But it wouldn't fix the Resource Gap. So he created the boy, the first of his kind, as far as we know. A genetic super weapon. Once activated with a recombinant, his DNA uses a process similar to steganography and becomes viral-like and airborne. Little stegs of genetic data embed themselves in the people around him and start to exploit vulnerabilities within their own genetic code. They begin to die from natural causes at an unnatural rate."

"That sounds complicated and slow," Tyler said. "Cullings are simple and fast."

The kid tried to sit up, but a soldier pressed him back to the table.

He called, "Mr. Tyler?"

"Say you were going to die of a heart attack at age sixty," Sara said. "Now maybe you have it at twenty-four. Alzheimers at ninety? You're forgetting your name at nineteen. The average lifespan wherever he is drops by decades, but nobody knows why or maybe even notices. And that's the point."

"Mr. Tyler, please, let's go." The kid turned to the soldier, "Let me sit up, okay?" The soldier helped him up.

Tyler looked at the boy. That was how he worked? He made people sick? An emotional coin was flipping within him; on one side, frustration that the kid wasn't a bomb or something spectacular that would make a statement, that his mission may be for nothing. On the other…relief?

"You're disappointed," Sara said. "You were hoping for something grander. Indeed he does have an overclock function."

The kid grunted, holding his stomach, then vomited between his knees. Pieces of venison and bile slapped onto the plastic.

"Ma'am," said one of the men in the green smocks.

"We're out of time," Sara said. "SLS built in a military application to make the contract with LCP more robust. We don't know how the overclock key works, but we do know that Staern keeps it on himself at all times. As far as we can tell, if the boy's triggered, he'll dissolve any living material within a hundred meters in every direction."

"How do you know all this?"

"We were skating SLS's optic channels looking for sweets."

"Okay, that."

"Sweets?"

"The overclock. That's what I'm going to do." In Tyler's heart, he felt a frantic flapping at the words, as if he were trying to herd them back. But why the guilt? The kid would be used to slaughter millions or be a pawn in some ridiculous revolution at best. The merciful thing would be a swift end. Tyler could be merciful. Couldn't he?

"Well, see, now we've come to the part where we decide if we can help each other. I need that boy, Tyler. The syncasts we can make with him, when we reveal this new weapon, that beautiful face, it'll be the end of all of them. The Big Seven CEOs will lose their grip on Thatcher and the LCP government. But I need the recombinant first. And I need to see if there are more Culls. Both of those things are inside SLS. Not an easy building to get into. I could sure use a soldier who knows a thing or two about incursions. A soldier like a JACKK."

Was her play-it-cool mask slipping? Tyler thought he saw something new beneath it, oily and putrid. "Seems like we're heading the same direction," Tyler said.

"Seems like."

"But the boy goes with me and we kill Staern."

"We can talk about that, but for now we have a general working agreement?" Sara asked.

Tyler never had any fucking choices. "For now."

"Ok. Next item. Did you know you're being tracked?"

"Yeah."

"It's an interstitial metafilament transponder — IMT. It's in his arm. We've been jamming the signal, but SLS has almost finished hacking us. The arm has to go."

Tyler thought about this for a moment, then said, "I saw a meat doctor, but he wouldn't do it."

"Good thing. Probably would have given the boy anesthesia and killed you all."

Tyler looked at Sara.

"The boy has a kill switch. Introduce anesthesia into his system and he melts down. Keeps people from reverse engineering him. Protect trade secrets and all that."

"You want to cut off his arm. Without anesthesia."

"If we had time, we could syncast over the pain, maybe, but as you said...on a clock."

She waved and the soldier who'd been standing behind Tyler came around and unlocked his handcuffs.

"You're strong." Sara took Tyler by the elbow as they walked towards the kid. "Might be best if you hold the arm."

The boy was hunched over, his elbows resting on his knees as he sat at the edge of the steel table. He looked up at Tyler. How much had he heard? Tyler couldn't tell. He tried to slow Sara's pace. Not so fast. Let him think for a minute.

"You know the crazy thing about that Kibashi girl?" Sara asked. "Two weeks later her old man hangs himself in his penthouse. The syncast she recorded of herself burning to death on loop. I guess he couldn't stand the idea that he'd done that to his own daughter."

The cackle of the plastic tarp. The slap of waves from the wharf. The rattle of the child's shaking body as he was forced back on the steel table echoing the rattle of Tyler's heart. These were the sounds he heard, or imagined hearing. He knew there was a line somewhere here. He couldn't see it, but he knew once crossed, he couldn't be who he had been any longer, he couldn't wrap himself in those gentle lies any longer.

"Please," said the boy after Tyler told him what was going to happen. "But how will I write my name? I'm sorry."

"Maybe we can just go," Tyler said to the woman. "What difference does it make if he sees us coming?"

"For whatever I am. I'm sorry."

"You think Staern'll just send a crawlbot and a couple of soldiers next time? Now that he knows a JACKK is escorting him?" She said it with a sympathetic smile on her face. Another mask to hide behind, this one of helplessness.

"I don't want my arm cut off," the boy said. His voice was climbing.

"You think they'd even let the boy live? Obviously, they're controlling something inside of him."

One of the surgeons pulled his cart closer.

The boy looked at the saws on it. "Oh, please, sir," he said to the soldier who'd been guarding him since they arrived. "Help me."

"Maybe the Twitcher is right," the soldier said.

Sara turned a furious glare on the man. "Go," she said. The soldier shrugged and walked toward one of the parked vans.

"Let's go," she said to the surgeon.

"No," the boy shouted. "No!" He tried to sit up, but Tyler held him down.

"Please, Mr. Tyler." He whispered, the words spilling out, desperate, chasing each other. "I'll do anything you want and if they're tracking me, I'll run and I'll lead them away from you so you can go and hurt Mr. Staern and I'll hide and they'll never find me and then you can sneak in and nobody will know you're coming because they'll think you're with me, but I'll be hiding and they won't be able to find me because I'm really good at hiding, I hide all the time and even ask Mr. Fahrs, he said I was good at hiding when a logging-bot almost saw me. Please, please, please." The last pleases were little more than cracks.

Tyler could feel the thwump, thwump of the kid's heart, the scattered, seizing breaths, the rigid terror. He tried to remind himself that this boy was designed for killing, that if Staern had his way, the boy would massacre tens, even hundreds of thousands, including other children just like him, who would never have a chance to beg for their lives. He tried to remind himself that within two days' time, the boy would be dead anyway and then he wouldn't feel any of this.

He tried to remind himself to not care.

"I was in a scary time once when I was your age, too," Tyler said. He brushed back the boy's sweaty hair, then rested his hand on the boy's head. "My mom put her hand on my head kind of like this and said that no matter what happens from this day forward, never let someone see you shake, no matter how scared you might be. Stand up tall, she said. Show them who you are."

Snot bubbled out of the kid's nose as he cried. He wasn't gasping, or wailing anymore. He lay quiet in his suffering.

The surgeon sliced his scissors up through the Together in Hope shirt.

"Why?" the boy whispered. "I don't want to hurt anyone. Why can't everyone just let me go?"

"Pain is a part of life," Tyler said. "All you can do is breathe and wait for it to go away."

"Please, mister. Pretty please."

"It'll be okay." When had it become so easy to lie? "Retreat forward, kid."

"No," the boy screamed. "No! No! No!" He bucked his hips and tried to kick.

"Hold him," the surgeon snapped.

"It'll go faster, if you hold still, you little shit," the soldier holding his legs said.

"Don't talk to him like that," Tyler growled. They locked eyes, but there was no debate who would blink first.

"Just breathe, kid," Tyler said.

"Save the fistula," Sara said. "We'll need that for the recombinant."

The surgeon inserted the scalpel several centimeters below the port on the kid's elbow. Blood pooled and cut tiny rivulets down his soft skin.

"Owy, owy, owy," the boy gasped. "Oh God, please stop."

Tyler closed his eyes.

"Please," the boy screamed.

When Tyler opened them again he saw the back of Sara as she

walked away. So that was the kind of woman she was. Tyler felt he had her measure now.

Cords of muscle bunched and contracted like spasming snakes in the kid's arm. Desperation makes men powerful, Tyler thought. Even boys.

"I hate you!" The boy began gasping. "I hate—"

The doctor finished his initial incisions and began peeling back the skin and muscle tissue.

If Tyler thought the boy had been crying before, he wasn't prepared for the sounds the boy made now. His ears dampened the wails to protect his hearing.

The boy spasmed and vomited a spray of yellow bile. It lanced across the Silent Uprising soldier holding his shoulders.

"Son of a—" the soldier jumped back.

The boy coughed and spit several times. "I hate you. I hope you all die. I hope everyone dies!"

A salty spurt of blood hit Tyler in the mouth.

"Shit," the surgeon said.

Tyler looked down. That was a lot of blood.

The surgeon was moving faster now, his fingers deft, but edging on panic.

The boy stopped screaming and his arm went soft. He'd lost consciousness.

After a few seconds the doctor let out his breath. "Okay," he said. "Saw."

The assistant handed him a small saw with a circular blade. It hummed when he flipped the switch forward. "Get the pump ready."

The assistant lifted the glass canister and pulled out a tube with a black suction cup looking thing from inside of it.

"What is that?" Tyler asked.

"Hold the arm. He might wake."

The doctor lowered the saw into the opening and Tyler could see the boy's bones. The radius was all white, but the ulna was black from the webbing wrapped around it. The saw cut into the bone with a whine two or three centimeters away from the sheath.

Moments later, the arm was free and the doctor handed it

to his assistant. The man attached the black suction sleeve onto the amputated end, closed it in the glass case, then pressed some buttons on the base of it. A second later the assistant nodded and handed the case to another soldier who had approached during the procedure.

"It's pumping. You've got thirty, maybe forty hours," the assistant said.

Meanwhile, the surgeon was grinding off the ends of the bones, smoothing them out. Tyler watched as the doctor finished stitching the muscles over the ends of the bones, then folded the skin over that.

"Normally, we'd have the cybernetics ready to attach," the doctor said. "We'd be here another couple hours shaping muscles and getting blood vessels and nerves ready to couple, but no need for that today, is there? Kind of nice doing a surgery where you don't have to give a damn."

"Doctor," Tyler said.

"I'm just saying, if you know the house is going to burn down in a couple days, you don't bother fixing the broken windows. Am I right?"

"Doc, look at me," Tyler said. "Finish this without another word, or I will use that saw to make you into a woman."

"But—"

Tyler cocked his head.

The doctor looked back at his work.

Once the doctor was bandaging the arm, Tyler let go and straightened up. He wondered if the boy would live. He wondered if there was an answer to that question that he should hope for.

They were in the back of a van traveling to the Silent Uprising's base. The boy lay unconscious, a blanket folded between him and the steel rivets. Tyler watched as the boy's chest rose and fell, his bandaged half-of-an-arm taped to his body. He could still taste the boy's blood on his lips. Could taste his sins writ across his own mouth. The sins of a man against a boy whose only crime was being what someone made him to be.

Tyler tried not to throw up.

A
REVOLUTION

He remembered her being beautiful. Even then, at seven, he knew she was beautiful. She had long brown hair that was almost black. It swept around the cables and reflected the lights of the synmap deck and the neon HDK logo hanging on the building outside their cubit's window. He'd sit on his cradle and watch the blinking lights, scarlet and violet and azure. Words he'd learned in a syncast, he was sure. She was under, of course. She always was, but not him. It had stopped working for him and she kept taking his Seven Ten, but that was okay because he didn't really like the 'casts and without the Seven Ten it made his tummy feel yucky, but she liked it so she should have it. He wanted her to have it.

He wondered if she remembered his name.

For the Lower Skims, the hospital bay was beyond anything Tyler had ever seen. Six beds, each with a white backing wall that curved up and over the patient, lined one side of the room looking towards a wall of windows on the other. The smart surfaces could display images during surgery or convert to lights or heat lamps as needed. There was enough room between each for a separate cradle connected to synmaps and blood bots and a number of other machines Tyler didn't recognize. The blood bot was good news. He'd be able to run a cycle of dialysis and maybe win back a couple of hours. Maybe help his body recover. His leg had stopped bleeding, but the bullets hadn't yet come out of either his leg or his abdomen.

The boy was in the farthest bed from the door, laying on his side with his back to Tyler. A window looked into the hallway across from him and the wall over the kid was lit up with ticking and waving biometrics, a life defined, but not understood.

"Hey," he said.

The boy didn't move.

Tyler walked around the foot of the bed and saw that the boy's eyes were open. He looked at Tyler, then rolled the other way so his back was to him again. The boy winced when he moved his amputated arm. They had wrapped a Hopkins Numball gel casing around the end of it for cushion and to kill any pain, but they hadn't bothered with acceleration strips. After all, if the house is going to burn down, you don't fix the windows.

"I brought you a Nangnang Bar," Tyler held the candy bar out to the kid. "They have solids here. Lots of them."

The kid didn't move.

"The gel helping the pain?"

Silence. How many times had Tyler told the kid to shut up on the drive to Cerebus? Careful what you wish for, his mom would have said. He was pretty sure she had never learned the rest of the idiom.

"Alright," Tyler said. He started to walk away.

"You're right," the boy said. "They are."

Tyler turned to him.

"People. They really are mean."

"Yeah, kid. They are."

"So is the fat woman."

"Sara. Yeah."

"When you get into Mr. Staern's tower," the boy said, "once you get what you need, you'll kill her, right? When you get what you need."

Tyler inhaled and held a deep breath. This wasn't a question the boy would have asked four hours ago.

"You don't mean that."

"You'll kill her, right?" The kid was staring at him. Hard. "You'll have to. She'll ruin everything if you don't."

Where did this come from? Tyler thought about the violence the child had seen in the last two days.

His eye hurt. The lights felt too bright, too honest.

"Yeah. I guess."

"You promise?"

He was dizzy and his thoughts wobbled. He wanted to sit down.

"Yeah, kid," he said. "I promise."

"On your life," the kid said and rolled over. Tyler's head started to clear.

***

Tyler looked at his watch again. -01:08:20:08. How had he lost so much time? He'd only been talking to the boy for ten minutes, but his watch was saying he'd lost a half hour.

He was standing on a mezzanine watching Silent Uprising soldiers drill incursion tactics. Blue, circuited tape had been used to grid out the walls and doorways of Staern Tower on the floor. Tyler knew it was interacting with the soldiers' synmaps right now, simulating the walls and interiors for the soldiers just as real as being in the space.

And what the fuck is the dizziness about? He'd almost lost his shit and fallen over in by the kid. Was this early denouement? He needed to try dialysis again and they needed to fucking hurry with this plan.

As he turned to leave, he noticed Sara approaching.

"Have a minute?" She smiled and touched him on his arm.

"Not many," Tyler said.

She leaned over the railing and watched the silent dance of the soldiers. All of their guns' sound effects and communications were handled through the synmaps, so that the only physical sounds they made were the squeaks of boots on the polished floor.

"Skimmers. Every one," she said.

"They're disciplined."

"Get someone off Seven Ten and the smack they sling in those sacs and you'll be surprised what they can do."

"What are we waiting for?"

"Our ride through the Veil is on its way down the Little Marek. Couple hours yet. Not long."

Sara turned around and leaned back against the railing. Tyler couldn't help but notice the shape of her breasts under her jacket. She wasn't so fat, just soft. Even with the greying hair. It had been a while since he'd seen a woman up close not counting the vet tech back in Wisconsin.

"We need to talk about your plan," she said.

"Pretty simple. You get me into SLS, I do the killing your soldiers can't, we get the boy's recombinant, I take him from there to get his overclock key and you guys do…whatever it is you're

planning to do."

"And you blow up the kid and Malcolm Staern?"

Does he blow up the kid and Malcolm Staern? Was that still his plan? Tyler saw the boy's face, saw him laying on the van's floor, his amputated arm bouncing against his small body.

"Doesn't matter to you what happens from there," Tyler said.

"But it does. Very much. You're thinking too small Tyler the JACKK. That boy could be invaluable to us."

"Get one of the other Culls they're making."

"We don't know there are others. We think maybe that's why Staern is so desperate."

"The boy goes with me."

Sara smiled and touched his arm again, this time on his forearm, just above the watch. On his skin.

"Hear me out. We are at a crossroads, Tyler. For generations, ever since the Great Divestment and the start of the Resource Gap, Skimmers have been turned into drugged out zombies and kept alive out of some sense of duty. Just enough moral anguish to keep the LCP from wholesale slaughter of two-hundred million people, but not enough moral anguish to avoid selective slaughter of a couple hundred thousand every ten years or so."

"Lady, I've heard all the arguments. Saving us from extinction, from the biologists. Cathartic release, from the psychs. Virtually eliminated crime, from the pigs. But I'll tell you what, ask the seven-year-old me if he felt it was cathartic or if he felt stopping petty theft was worth getting torched to ashes for and you probably would've gotten the middle finger."

"Exactly my point. What do the Skimmers say? Even that name. Skimmers. Dehumanize them just enough so you can tell yourself it's okay."

"Sure. Now ask the twenty-seven year-old me if he gives a shit about any of that and you'll probably get this." Tyler flipped her the bird.

Sara held up her hand. "Charming. My point is, all of that is changing. The Big Seven corporate sponsors of the LCP are afraid. They know they've taken too much power from the government, basically are the government. And they can sense the people rising up. Not Skimmers, but High Laners. The actual doers of society. Tyler, the boy could be the thing that pushes it all over the edge. First, his existence will undermine SLS's claim that the Cullings can be ended. And second, we can use him to kill off the families of the Big Seven. Topple them from the top down."

"Listen," Tyler said. "Half of what you said is old news, the other half is someone else's fucking problem. I don't give two shits about you and your crusade or Skimmers. As far as I care, when I die the rest of the world can die, too. The boy is my way out of here and my way of taking the one fucking man who deserves it the most with me."

"You're doing right for all of the wrong reasons," Sara said.

"You're not listening. I don't care about your right and wrong."

"Have you ever seen what happens in a Culling?" Sara asked. "Not the sanitized LCP version, but what really happens?"

The flash of the personal incinerators. Tyler's skin on his face tightening from the heat, fake feeling, like a mask. A mask to hide behind. Hiding. "Oh." Her half-hearted whisper as the flames tornadoed around her.

"Tyler," Sara said.

He stepped back from her, finding himself on the mezzanine again. "We're done here," he said.

"Work with me, Tyler. I usually get what I want."

"You sound like the kid. Every time I don't do what he demands he throws a fit."

"Tyler," Sara said, an edge on her voice. "It'll be easier if I can trust you."

Tyler grunted and doubled over, gripping Sara's shoulders for support. It felt like an animal was clawing its way out of his side where he'd been shot. He lifted his shirt and caught the 9mm slug as it squeezed out of his body. That had taken hours longer than normal, but he was glad it was out.

Sara took his hand in hers and turned it so she could see the bullet. "That's amazing," she said. "Did that just come out of you?"

Tyler felt frozen, his hand being held by hers.

She looked up at his face, going from his Sakanaya to his flesh eye. "I've read time moves slower for Twitchers. That the amphetamines and other drugs they have you on make you intensely aware."

She stepped closer and gently, slowly pulled his shirt up to see his wound. It was a pink, puckered scar, already closed by the nanocellotics, like the end of a tied balloon. Dried blood crusted around it. Sara traced her fingertips around the wound, then up over his belly.

"You're strong," she whispered. "Hard."

"Stop."

"We have time. I wonder what a Twitcher would be like. Too fast? Too slow?" Her face came within centimeters of his, her lips open. "Too big?"

Tyler pushed her away. "I only want one thing from you," he said. "You're getting me past the Veil and into SLS. From there the boy and Malcolm Staern are mine. At that point, you can go fuck yourself for all I care."

Sara snatched her hand away from him. "None of this would be happening without me and I know what it's going to take to get to the next level. What the sacrifices will be. That Kibashi girl? She didn't just wake up one day and decide to set herself on fire. That took months of work. I have worked too hard, waited too long for this opportunity to see some Twitcher toss it all away in meaningless revenge."

"It means everything to me." Tyler walked away.

"Nobody will care," Sara shouted. "Nobody will even notice you're dead."

The thing that held soldiers back for centuries was their humanity. They needed things like food and rest and objectives. Purpose. The JACKK was developed to satisfy almost all of their physical needs, all but eliminating the need for sleep and food to only a couple times a week. Amphetamines, analgesics, steroids; these things trickled through Tyler's system every second of every day for the last six years. However, it wasn't the amphetamines keeping him awake now as he lay on a cot they'd given him. It wasn't the noise of the soldiers moving through the hallway outside or the clatter in the pipes running up the wall next to him. It was the image of the boy, his half-arm pointing at Tyler like an accusation.

Tyler hurt everywhere. He couldn't remember ever hurting this bad. He looked at his watch. -01:07:57:21 Less than thirty-two hours until he would die. Leave the world behind forever. Tyler had read about religion, knew there were still some people, maybe in the High Lanes, that believed that stuff. Part of Tyler wished he could. He wanted to know there was something, anything, after he died, that these twenty-seven years he had weren't all of it. If they were and this is what he had done with them, what would that say about him as a person? Look at the shit he'd done. The lives he'd ended or ruined. From what he understood, that next step, if it existed, was a doozy, with some rigid requirements on how you treated others for getting in. If that were the case, Tyler figured he'd have a better chance of getting into Heaven simply because Hell would be too full.

The boy only had thirty-two hours, also. Less, in fact. Pisser of it was, he didn't know it. Not exactly. Not to the second, like Tyler. Tyler had spent the last six years getting used to the idea of dying, watching his time literally tick away. The boy, through no fault of his own, was also on that clock now, but hadn't been given ample warning. What was that like, Tyler wondered. How mad would Tyler be if someone was doing this to him? He wouldn't forgive it, Tyler knew. If he were in the kid's spot, he'd do whatever he could to get revenge on the people who put him there, including Malcolm Staern.

Staern. There's a man Tyler wished he could send a watch to that was counting down and say, "time is running short." Let that asshole sweat the bullet that can't be stopped. Or, in this case, the Culling.

She was sitting there on the boy's cot talking when Tyler came into the medical bay. The Silent Uprising woman and the boy. Laughing even. Tyler had never seen the boy laugh before. That look on his face as he was laughing, searching Sara's face for signs that she was sharing his joy. That word alone, joy. Tyler couldn't think of a time he'd ever spoken or even thought that word until now.

Everything in him was miserable and sore after sleeping, so it was part hurt feelings and part simply just hurt that bumped along under the words when he said, "Look at you suck-bunkies. Getting along now?"

"We were just talking about you," Sara said.

"Funny, I wasn't even thinking about you."

"Ben was talking about the woods you lived in. I wonder, whose manners were affected more out there, yours or the animals?" She stood and straightened the blankets she had been sitting on, then patted the boy's leg and said, "You don't need to worry about anything."

She didn't look at Tyler as she left.

Tyler rolled over the blood bot over and sat in the cradle next to the boy. He snapped the coupler to the port in his left arm.

"You guys looked chummy," Tyler said. "You still want what we talked about?"

A quick sequence on the bot's screen and he could feel the blood pulled out of him. He looked out the window as a male nurse with freckles walked past. The nurse glanced in at them, then jerked his gaze away when he saw Tyler.

"What are you doing?" the boy asked.

"Dialysis."

"Dal-sis?"

"Die-al-i-sis," Tyler enunciated. "I figured out that if I did this every couple of days, I'd buy back some time. It cleans the blood of some of the toxins from the JACKK."

"You get time back?"

"Not much anymore, but maybe some."

The kid watched the blood moving up the clear tube into the machine, then said, "Yes."

Tyler looked at the boy.

"She's mean. You all are."

Tyler's forced chuckle came out as a grunt. "Committed, kid. Just committed."

The freckled nurse shuffled in carrying bandages and tape to change the boy's dressing. Tyler noticed he was sweating and three times while cutting away the Numball gel he dropped the scissors, stuttering a cymbal staccato on the steel floor. Tyler had to look away when the bandages were finally removed and that savaged flesh glared its accusations at the world.

When the nurse was finished and left Tyler said, "Thought he was going to stab you with those scissors."

"I've never seen him before," the boy said.

They listened to the beep of the blood bot and the whispering of the pumps for a while.

"Is Mr. Staern mean? Is that why you hate him," the boy asked.

Reasons matter. Tyler knew this. Understanding why we do something before we do it changes how well we do that thing. Would telling the boy why he was going to die help the kid to die better? Was it maybe the least Tyler could do?

"You ever cast Bambi?"

"Maybe? It's old, right? About the deer and his mom getting killed?"

"Yeah. Only instead of nice bunnies and skunks taking care of the fawn, imagine drugged-out wolves who are as happy eating each other as anything else. Then imagine, when the wolves finally decide they're going to eat Bambi because the damn fawn is also now drugged-out and useless, the fawn finds the strength to kill a few wolves and run away, but where does he end up? Right back in the arms of the hunter that shot his mom. Only now, the hunter puts a collar on the fawn and shoots him up with more, different narcotics and cybernetics and the fawn turns into a buck and grows giant fucking antlers to stab people with. One catch, Big Buck has to stab who the hunter wants stabbed, isn't going to see his thirtieth birthday and, anyway, he never really wanted the antlers and he never really wanted his mom shot. He just wanted to be left alone."

"Mr. Staern killed your mom?"

The blond nurse walked past the window again, looking at the boy, then Tyler.

"He Culled her." It was only partly a lie.

"Is that when she said that thing to you? About being brave?"

"I didn't think you'd remember."

"How'd you get away?"

"We were in the kitchens when the doors were locked down." When do partial lies add up to a whole lie? "She shoved me into an oven. The insulated walls protected me from the incinerators they used. Dumb luck that we were up and in the kitchens. Everyone else was under the synmap."

The kid picked at his gel pack, squeezing suspended bubbles from one end to the other.

"People are terrible, aren't they?"

"Yeah."

"I used to think everyone was nice."

The blood bot beeped that it was finished. Tyler uncoupled the tube from his arm's port, then looked at his watch. -01:04:28:16 He netted thirty minutes. A damn half hour.

"They'll use you the second they can." He stood and let the tube drop into the cradle. "And when they're done, they'll toss you aside. If you're not looking out for yourself, don't think anybody else is. That's what I'd tell you if you were my kid, I guess."

"But I already figured that out, didn't I?"

"Yeah," Tyler said. "I guess you did."

Four magazines for his Mark 37 left. He loaded one into the gun and the other three he clipped into the pouches on the front of his combat vest. Three magazines for his MK-9. Again, one in the gun, two in his belt pouches. The melmoth shirt was a mess. Partial punctures and rusted blood riddled the armor from the barrage he'd taken at Cerebus, making it useless. He tossed it in the corner.

Then he saw the thetabiencort canister. The silver promise rested on his cot among his tools. He picked it up and turned it under the light and he could see himself reflected in the side of it, stretched and distorted and he thought that was appropriate.

What was he doing here? Everything hurt. Every tendon, every muscle, every bone, every thought. What did he think would happen when he killed Staern?

He turned the canister over and saw the outlet for the medicine, the valve waiting to be inserted into a plunger. He could do it. Send a cascade of poison spurting into his body. Sleep. Forget about

Staern Life Sciences and Cullings and nanocellotics. Forget about time. Never look at a watch again. There was appeal in giving up. Retreat backwards, for once. Who would judge? Like Sara said, who would even notice?

But someone would notice, wouldn't he? Because what would happen to him?

If Tyler died now, what would happen to the boy?

***

Doing what Tyler had done for six and a half years for the LCP, he knew the sounds of panic, as clear as a bird's trill. He jammed the rest of his gear into his backpack. Sara appeared at his door, her hair pasted to her shining forehead.

"Ben's gone," she said, breathless. "A nurse took him."

Tyler slung his assault rifle over his shoulder and was in the hallway before she finished speaking. A nurse. That sweaty, clumsy bastard. Tyler was furious at himself for not recognizing the signs.

"When?"

They reached the ladders and began taking the rungs two at a time. It made Tyler crazy how slow everyone moved.

"Minutes. The barge isn't long now. We went to get him ready to move and he was missing. Holoscanners showed everything three, four minutes ago."

The Silent Uprising base had been converted from an underground refinery, seven stories of operations well hidden from LCP satellites. Seven stories doesn't sound like much until you are waiting for twenty fat-ass soldiers and an old lady to climb ladders all while your kid is being taken by a strange man. Wait. Your kid? The hell.

Out of the silo, surfacing in a hangar-like building. The hangar housed the SU's fleet, a couple of shiny sedans, Mercedes, if Tyler wasn't mistaken, seven Ford Crusades, those utility jeeps with the gatling mounts and twelve white vans. Twelve vans. Tyler had counted thirteen when they had arrived.

"Can you track it?" Tyler asked.

Sara shook her head.

Amateurs.

Two squads of ten men had followed them.

"We're splitting up," Tyler said.

Sara tossed him a throat mic. "This is scrambled."

Tyler plugged the mic into his synport as he sprinted full-tilt after the kid. His heart was pounding and he felt the familiar flow of juice from his JACKK, but something tainted it. It was weaker than normal and his chest hurt where the kit's distributor cap was embedded.

Outside, squinting against the midday sun, Tyler scanned the oil field. Four minutes wasn't much of a head start. If Tyler were a betting man (and right now all the chips were on the table), he'd bet they'd head for Ribic Lane, then onto the Byway.

He crossed the service road into Water Well, the suburb butting up to the refinery. The buildings here were taller, six or seven story structures, mostly residence towers. He would be able to hop scotch between them. Using a combination of fire escapes and power conduit, he shimmied up one of the buildings, then chased from one end to the other looking for the van. Nothing.

Four minutes. Traveling sixty, seventy kilometers per hour max on these shit roads. That puts them four-ish kilometers out. He should be able to spot them from here. What if those dumb crusader fucks didn't read the clock right? What if it had been more than four minutes?

He vaulted from rooftop to rooftop as he raced north along Third Way. There. Half a kilometer ahead. They were heading to the Three-twenty on-ramp. Tyler could cut them off at Fifth and Ribic if he didn't miss a beat.

Tyler started coughing when he landed on the eighth rooftop and had to stop and hold onto a ventilation pipe. He felt like he'd swallowed a campfire. Was this it? He looked at his watch. Twenty-three hours left. Not for the first time, he wondered if it could be wrong.

He was running again. The next building was several stories taller than the one he was on and he had to leap onto someone's patio. He plowed into the plastic doors, then pried them open. Inside a man lay naked in his cradle, plugged into a synmap and IV. He didn't move at the sounds. Tyler tore through his unit and into the hallway. Up the stairs to the roof again.

Four more jumps—his lungs hauling breaths in and out, his knees and heels throbbing—and he was in assault position on the van turning onto Ribic. He swung his Mark 37 up to his shoulder, barely allowing his Sakanaya to provide a targeting solution before firing. He emptied his clip into the engine, pieces of radiator and plastic and fiberglass sparkling in the sun. The van lost control, rolled on its side and shrieked along the pavement, wedging itself against the far building.

The passenger door popped like a hatch. A woman with strawberry hair and blood across her forehead braced her wrists in the hinge of the door and fired. She was fast—one of the soldiers, then—but Tyler was faster. He dropped the Mark 37, unholstered his sidearm, railed out and fired twice. Just as her first bullet powdered against the concrete facade at Tyler's feet, his two shots entered her forehead above her left eye. The splatter rounds confettied the back of her skull.

Breathe. Breathe. Slow your breathing. The boy was still in there. He had to be okay, Tyler told himself.

After a full two seconds of watching the driver's side, scanning for thermal images and finding nothing, Tyler climbed down the building, holding his MK-9 on the driver's side the entire way.

Once on the street, he crept around the bottom of the tipped van, the axels and drive train exposed, raw and impotent. The back hatch was open, one door swung fully around to rest on what was now the roof of the van, the other on the street like a ramp. The nurse knelt on what used to be the inside wall, holding a gun to the boy's head.

"It's too late," the nurse said. "I already called. They're coming."

Tyler sighted on the nurse's face. The man's trigger finger was tense. Too tense.

"Let the kid go," Tyler said.

"They're taking me into the High Lanes. I've earned it. If you want to live, run."

"Mr. Tyler," the boy said. "He's also mean."

Tyler's arm twitched as he held it straight out. He tried to use his cybernetic arm to steady it, but he could see the barrel randomly moving a half-degree off target. That had never happened before. How certain could he be of his next shot?

"Kill him," the boy said. That was two. Two people now the boy had asked Tyler to kill. A hollowing out happened somewhere inside Tyler's belly. Sure, they both deserved it, but the requests from the kid?

"You're a nurse, right," Tyler said.

"Shut up," he said. His freckles were blazing, panicked blood flushing his face.

"So you get how funny adrenaline is," Tyler said. "How it shoots you full of cortisol which sends your lungs into overdrive."

"I'll kill him if I have to."

"This gets more oxygen to your ticker and your ticker goes crazy getting that oxygen everywhere it needs to go. Thing is, everywhere it needs to go doesn't include your brain. The good ol' prefrontal cortex doesn't help you fight or flight, right? So it gets a little oxygen starved when you're stressed." Tyler needed to get the nurse to slacken his grip on the pistol, release the trigger from the breaking point, so any dying spasm wouldn't accidentally set off the gun.

"You're not thinking clearly," Tyler said. "It's not your fault. Your brain is doing the best it can with what it's getting, but right now, you think holding a gun to the tumor SLS is coming to pick up is a good idea. And you think a JACKK can't shoot you before you can kill the kid."

The nurse lifted his face from behind the boy to glare at Tyler and said, "I've thought it all thr-"

Tyler's gun bellowed its final argument, the roar echoing inside the van. The man slumped forward, blood baptizing the kid.

The boy scrambled out from under the dead nurse and ran to Tyler and gave him a one-armed hug, burying his face in Tyler's stomach. He was shaking, but not crying. Silent. Tyler lifted his arms as if he were afraid to touch the boy. He looked at the kid, unsure of what to do. This was the first time in two years he'd been touched by another person not trying to kill him. Sure Sara had tried her pass at him, but that was pure manipulation. This was... more. More honest. More innocent. More...right.

He lowered a hand to rest on the boy's head. His hair was full of the nurse's blood.

The kid let go, stepped back and looked at Tyler. Those were not the boy's eyes, Tyler knew. Those were not the eyes of the boy he had found in his cabin.

"If you can be counted on for anything it's that, right? Why have antlers if you're not going to stab people?" the boy said. "And don't call me tumor. My name is Ben." He walked away.

Tyler looked at the dead nurse in the back of the van, slumped over himself as if praying. He looked at his shirt where the kid had hugged him. At the bloodstain the kid's hug had left. At the echo of violence.

"It's over," Sara said.

They stood, Tyler, the kid, Sara and her two squads of soldiers on top of one of the buildings Tyler had just crossed in his chase. Four kilometers away, SLS drones, Crawlbots and LCP police were laying waste to the Silent Uprising's headquarters. A cacophony of heavy assault weapons and mechanized devastation skittered through the streets.

"We can't go on," Sara said. Her wet eyes reflected the explosions. "We have to call off the assault."

"No," Tyler said.

"No," the boy said.

Both Tyler and Sara looked at the boy. His hair was matted into brown, bloody clumps and his amputated arm was bleeding, the bandages soaked through and tattered.

"I want to see Mr. Staern," the boy said.

"He thinks he won," Tyler said. "It'll take time for them to know if the boy is in there."

"Two squads isn't enough."

"I'll do it alone, then."

"No," the boy said. "Together."

Together? Not twenty-four hours ago the child was begging to run. When had this happened? Tyler couldn't help but think something had broken in the child, that Tyler had broken it.

"Get us through the Veil," Tyler said.

"You think you're that good?" Sara looked at the bloodstains in his shirt and pants from being shot, the stains from the kid's hug. "You don't look that good."

As if to put the lie to Sara's words, Tyler's guts knotted on themselves and it took all of his strength not to let his legs go out from under him. Nausea swept upwards from his core. He checked his watch. -00:22:21:42 It was officially starting, Tyler knew. Twitcher Denouement.

While Tyler caught his breath, the drones and LCP police retreated from the Silent Uprising's base, falling back several blocks. Once safely away, a red light congealed above them, cutting through the night's clouds. It splashed crimson across all of Water Well as it lanced through the warehouse deep underground. A plume of dirt and debris rocketed into the air. A second later the sound of the explosion reached them.

"An orbital strike," Sara said. "What were we thinking?"

Once Tyler could breathe, the pain easing, he said, "You haven't seen anything yet."

They had summoned a dry-bulk cargo barge down the Little Marek, its shipping containers stacked three high and pulled by a Stetson Allen Escort Tug. Even with three azimuth thrusters, to

Tyler it felt as if they were swimming through wet concrete. Of the sixty containers, fifty-nine were filled with oats, soy beans and corn from Cerebus West.

That last one? Twenty-two armed men and women escorting a child home so they could kill his father.

It would be three hours to the Veil. At first, Tyler and the boy had taken turns peaking through the camoflaps masking the ingress ports, but it hadn't taken long for the boy to grow bored. Now he slept, his head on Tyler's shoulder. Tyler listened to the slight whistle from the boy's breathing, his lower lip shining with drool.

The boy's amputated arm lay across Tyler's lap, capped with a hard-case over the Numball gel. What bandages were visible were stained. Tyler examined his own flesh arm, his intravenous port and the lines of the JACKK system buried just beneath the skin, the purple, drug riddled veins like rivers in a pale desert. His heart hadn't slowed below a hundred beats per minute for the last hour and the pain he felt told him that whatever meds his kit had were either all used up or no longer effective. Whispers of death.

"He's sleeping?" Sara settled next to Tyler, their backs against the wall. The other SU soldiers had given Tyler and the boy their space—lots of it—mostly huddling at the rear of the container.

"I guess," Tyler said.

Sara nodded, then, acting cool about it, said, "By now, you must have recognized how important Ben is to us." Like that. Not a question.

"Sure," Tyler said. "I recognize it."

"Good. I'm glad to hear that." The chick didn't buy it, Tyler could tell. Too savvy for that. Give her anything, give her a sharp nose for bullshit.

"But he's going with me." And what happens to him from there is entirely my choice, Tyler thought.

"Tyler. An orbital strike, for the love of God."

"Yep."

"He's our ace. You have to know that. Without him...after today...I can't even think about it."

"You'll need to, because you aren't getting him."

"One man! You would waste him to kill one man, when I would use him—he would help us—liberate and save the lives of millions? People you might even know who are going to die in eight years. For what? For High Laners? Sooner if they start releasing Culls like Ben into the population. You would let this once-in-three-generations possibility slip through our fingers? For revenge? Stupid, meaningless revenge?"

She was shaking, her whisper unable to contain her frustration.

Would he kill the boy for revenge? This child with flaking blood from the nurse still in his hair?

"You give a whole lot of shits about a whole lot of people who don't give any for you. Because they don't. They don't give a shit about anything or anyone that doesn't come through a syncast or start with the number seven and end with ten. What's a High Laner like you care? Who crowned you 'Skimmer Savior?'"

"Who else will, Tyler? Don't they have a right—the most fundamental right of all—to live? They have no representation, nobody looking out for them, and even if they did, they aren't allowed awake long enough to complain to someone. Yeah. I give a shit."

"Then what? Stop the Cullings? Resource Gap doesn't go away. Skimmers aren't going to wake up and find a bunch of jobs that don't exist and learn how to farm on land so radiated your nads turn to watermelons. You folks didn't start this because you're a bunch of sick fucks like killing people in their sleep. You going to let everyone starve to death? Do you know what happens when people are hungry? I've operated in the Midlands. They don't sit in their huts waiting to die."

"I can't believe I'm hearing this. You think the Cullings are justified."

At that point, Tyler would have agreed to anything as long as it was the opposite of what this over-privileged, over-fed horse wanted.

"Maybe they are."

He instantly regretted the words. He swallowed, opened his mouth to speak, closed it.

"Kill them all," Sara said, really looking at him now. She'd done something with her anger, put it someplace, and what remained were green eyes that were almost steel-grey.

"You want fair."

Sara shook her head and picked at the fingernail on her left thumb. Purple dirt under the nail. They could feel the hum of the tug boat.

"All I have left is to beg, Tyler. Please. I am begging for the lives of millions. Don't take Ben with you up to Staern's after you get the recombinant. We could do more good with him than killing ten Malcolm Staerns would."

Not a horse. A fucking pit-bull.

"Look, maybe you can take the recombinant and any other Culls we find in the lab." Over his dead body. She'd be dead by then, anyway. Anything to get her to shut up. "But the boy goes with me."

They held each others' eyes for a long time.

"Sure," Sara said. She pushed against the wall to stand.

"And it's not," Tyler said.

Sara straightened her jacket, stood waiting.

"My revenge. It's not meaningless."

She rejoined her team at the rear of the container.

When Tyler looked down at the boy, his eyes were open.

The six hours of crawling along the Little Marek until it met the Veil felt longer than the two years Tyler had spent living alone in the woods. Calling it a giant tent was too simple. Rather, it was as if a silk curtain had been draped over the High Lanes. Ultra-light spines arced thousands of meters into the sky, the material bowing between them in graceful dips. Hundreds of barges and airships overhead stood in line waiting for entry. Ahead the port opened for transports, the veil pulled back to allow ships through, then dropping closed behind them. The tugboat slowed on approach.

It was a second Cerebus Gate, Tyler thought. The first keeps out the Midlands. The second keeps out the lowlifes.

"Complete silence," Sara whispered.

Everyone huddled, wrapping their cloaks and arms around dangling metal that might clank.

Tyler tightened his grip on his Mark 37.

"What is it?" the boy whispered.

Twelve AI drones flew up to the barge and began methodically scanning each container's data panel while two gun ships hovered off starboard. Sixty seconds later, Tyler felt the tug begin pulling again.

It was only once they were through the Veil that Tyler understood why there was a Veil at all. At first, he thought the High Lanes had an odd, but pleasant smell, then he realized it was that, for the first time in his life, he wasn't smelling anything at all. No smoke from the Slag Belt in Michigan or the ever-burning forest fires in the Midlands. No detritus rot.

Even with the material filtering it, the setting sunlight seemed somehow brighter, purer, more honest. He blinded his Sakanaya eye with his palm. The colors! Reds brighter than blood. Blues so rich he could drink them.

But nothing prepared him for the people. So many people. Talking. Shopping. And their clothes. Brands and styles he'd only ever seen in syncasts, like Cülo Smart Cloaks that reshaped themselves based on thousands of templates (additional purchase required) or Haggemeister Handbags with exclusive self-selecting feed system ("Search No More").

The number of people was unnerving. How would you know whom to watch out for? Who was dangerous and who wasn't? Some of them rode in wooden rickshaws, canvas tarps over the top. Tyler had heard that High Laners would bring a lucky few Skimmers up to do tasks like that, that they liked having humans do work that robots could easily do. It got the Skimmers into the High Lanes and gave them the one thing they never imagined having, a job. And hell, it seemed only fair that a human might steal back a robot's job. After all, hadn't they stolen enough from us leading up to the Great Divestment?

Holograms spun up and took form across every skyscraper Tyler could see. Advertisements for clothing and restaurants, companies and brands he'd never heard of. LSM Insurance. Liberty Conglomerate Bank ("Funding Dreams, Industry and Freedom"). Aero-Sail ("The Future of Transportation").

And food carts. It was as if nobody used nutrient sacs here, but instead wanted—could afford—solids every day.

He caught himself from cussing when he recognized his own face in one of the holograms. It was a LCNC newscast, the headline "Twitcher Terror at Cerebus Gate North" marching a perimeter around the building. A woman newscaster was speaking and with his Sakanaya's magnification he could read the subtitles. "…unclear, but it's suspected the assault was connected to recent terror operations aimed at extending the Resource Gap. With us to discuss is Dr. Emily Arenson, from the Resource Gap Policy Institute." The hologram cut from Tyler's face to a woman with blond hair and tiny cybernetic beads inserted around her cheek bones. A building passed in front of the hologram and when Tyler could read it again, the woman was saying, "…everything we possibly can to end the Cullings. Nobody, and I mean nobody, wants this tragic policy to continue any longer than it must. Unfortunately, the reality that instigated the need—the very stability of this last free nation in North America—hasn't changed. However, we are very close to a new solution…" The river turned and he could no longer see the news feed.

So that was how they were spinning it. Terror to extend the Resource Gap. It made sense. They couldn't hide the Cerebus attack. Too many High Laners worked there. Was this fame? Your face twenty meters tall? Millions of people now knew who he was. They thought he was changing their world, wrecking their status quo, even though he couldn't care less about their status or its quo. What would they think when he blew up one of the Big Seven CEOs? And used a yet-unheard-of weapon to do it. That last thought…it tasted like copper. Maybe murder was enough. Maybe the yet-unheard-of weapon wasn't necessary? Maybe it should be set free so it could stay unheard of?

The river made its final turn and this time Staern Tower rose, angular and enormous, ahead of them. A glass tooth so tall it seemed to chew at the Veil itself.

"Hey kid, there's Staern Tower," Tyler said, but the boy didn't answer.

He was staring at a father and son walking on the promenade.

The father looked at his son, laughing, then watched the passing barge. He seemed to be the same age as the kid and he carried a backpack while holding his father's hand.

The boy closed the camoflap, sat down and pulled his knees to his chest, wrapping his arms around his legs. He picked at the bandages on the stump of his left arm.

Tyler looked back at the father and son. It was the boy's left hand holding his father's.

From one container to another, this one a semi. Again in the back. Cargo on its way to Staern Tower. A package being delivered. A gift. But for whom?

Before the bay door was raised, the Silent Uprising soldiers had pulsed the waiting forklift and security drones with EMPs, then did the same to the remaining drones the receiving dock. Four of them wore adaptive camouflage.

Tyler knelt, shielding the boy with his body. As Sara and the other soldiers moved into the docking bay, Tyler stood to follow. Blackness strangled his vision to a pinhole, his injured leg buckling. He fell into the wall, grasping the cargo rack before he collapsed. The boy held Tyler's ammo belt with his one hand as if to catch him from falling.

"Are you coming?" Sara called.

"Don't give up now," the boy whispered. "You have a promise to keep."

Inside, Sara and the soldiers unfolded environmental suits from their backpacks and began pulling them on. They had painted their signature skull face with the "x" over the mouth on their ventilators. Sara looked at Tyler as she zipped hers up. Protection—they hoped—from the boy's steganography once triggered. "I figured you wouldn't need one," she said.

It wasn't like waltzing through a residence tower in the Lower Skims. Staern Tower was one-hundred-twenty-floors, the top ten locked down with genetic-marker keys. And it was no accident that the lab was on floor one-hundred-eleven. So, elevator to one-oh-nine (as high as it goes), running and gunning from there. That was okay with Tyler. Do a little killing on the way up. If there was anything Tyler was good at…and maybe a few S.U.s would eat it during the trip. Save Tyler some ammo once they found him the recombinant.

Tyler killed the elevator at one-oh-nine, popped the access hatch in the ceiling and pulled himself up. The plasma torch they handed him made quick work of the cinderblocks and ninety seconds later he had a one meter by one meter square cut into the stairwell, the scrap metal and concrete tucked quietly away in the elevator. Tyler had to admit, Sara's plan seemed solid. Bypass the doors' bio scanners by going through the wall.

The four soldiers in adaptive camo went in first, shimmering ghosts, followed by the remainder of the squad, Sara and finally the boy. By the time he got through the opening, Sara had connected a mimic box to the genetic sniffer on the lock to the upper levels. Impressive tech, even if it could only be loaded and used once.

"How are you doing this?" Tyler whispered. Access through the .Veil, adaptive camouflage, mimic boxes with Malcolm Staern's very own genetic signature—this was LCP spy shit.

"You haven't recognized me this whole time, have you?"

Tyler tried to place her, but nothing.

"LCP Senator Lemira. New England Ward," she said, holding out her hand as if to shake Tyler's. "Pleasure to meet you."

"A fucking senator."

The LED panel above the sniffer turned green and the door spiraled open.

"That's the last of my tricks." she said "From here on, it's every man for himself."

Close now and Tyler knew the kid could feel it. The way he was pinching his lower lip, his amputated arm hugging his ribs. Wretched, wracking fear.

This floor was bright. White molded plastic and shimmering chrome. Wayfinding screens woke as they passed, the stupid machines offering maps. "May I assist you in finding and killing my master?" No thanks. Got it covered.

Two minutes and three turns later they came to a massive room filled with bright colors and textured rugs. It sure didn't look like a lab. It looked like a fucking nursery. Children's toys, swirling patterns, color up and down the wall like splattered rainbows. On the far wall was what Tyler guessed was a two-way mirror and a door next to it.

The kid stopped at the window. He was looking at a cylinder robot balanced on a ball, wrapped with a padded display that could animate all types of monsters and fun creatures to attack. Knock it over and it bounces back, spins around you and eggs you on.

"I remember this room," the boy said.

Skimmers didn't get toys growing up, not many at least. They got tranquilizers until they could get ported and then they got dreams. Tyler did remember one toy his mother had given him—a cracked screen from a data pad some High Laner must have thrown away. Tyler would trace his finger across it, careful not to cut himself, imagining he were controlling armies of military drones in some assault. One time, he'd taped a string from the end of it to his synport behind his ear. Professional now. The real deal. When his mother saw she'd said, As if.

The door next to the two-way mirror opened and a woman in a blue and yellow lab coat walked through. She looked out the window and locked eyes with Tyler.

No contest, right? A middle-aged lady-nerd outrunning a Twitcher? In her dreams. Sometimes dreams do come true.

Tyler tried sprinting to the door into the nursery, but when his JACKK started pumping it felt as if the ninth gate of Hell had opened within his chest. He was sucking wind by the time he made it in, the woman long gone.

He kicked open the door she'd passed through and when he put down his leg, his knee was throbbing. In the side alleys of his mind, he was surprised to remember what being mortal was like.

It wasn't just her. It was her plus four. And he'd found the lab. A long room divided lengthwise by white cabinets and stainless steel countertops covered with microscopes, microarray scanners, tubes, bulbs and fume hoods. All the shit a company needs to warp kids into weapons of mass destruction.

Fuck this running stuff. Tyler skidded around the corner, raised his rifle and fired into the floor next to the woman. "Next one through your fucking skull," he shouted. One of the other lab techs screamed. The woman stopped running. Held her hands over her head.

Tyler was still panting when Sara walked up behind him. "I thought you were faster than that."

"Fuck off," he said.

The lab tech was on her knees, her fingers laced behind her head, when the kid walked up. She looked at him as if concussed, her eyes grey and scattered, then pulling together into frightened focus. "Ben?"

"Hello Ms. Kathy."

"Open it," Tyler said. They were at the back of the lab now, a stainless steel door standing between them and the recombinant. Fingerprints smeared across the surface.

Sara and the Silent Uprising soldiers held the other lab technicians at gunpoint, kneeling with their hands on their heads.

"You can't—" the woman started to say.

Tyler punched her in the stomach, catching her before she fell.

"Please, Ms. Kathy," the boy said. She'd said her name was Kathy Farris, Ph.D. in microbiology and genetic engineering from the Massachusetts Institute of Technology. Where Progress Can't Afford to Stop.

"He won't stop," the boy said.

Sara walked up behind Tyler. She'd been chatting—firmly— with the other four techs.

"The recombinant is in there," she said. The environmental suit gave her voice a robotic echo, her face hard to see behind the tinted visor.

"I know."

"The recombinant," Farris said. "How do you…"

"Please," the boy said.

The scientist found her balance and pulled herself free from

Tyler's grip. She stepped over to the door. The genetic sniffer scanned her face and when the light over the door turned from red to green, she said, "Ben, don't come in here."

Tyler had seen things in his life that to this day gave him nightmares, had done things no human should ever do to another human, but nothing had prepared him for what was in this lab. Was this what man was? Meat and sinew, engorged with blood and spastic efforts, but nothing of value? Rootless, vicious creatures? Tyler walked through the door and was surrounded by dead children.

Two dozen stainless steel autopsy tables stood in the room, with drains between them and children of all ages and sizes on them. Tyler walked down the center of the room, unable to think, one foot in front of the other. Infants, teenagers, fat, thin. That one couldn't be more than six-months old. That one, seven? Several were half dissected, their abdomens unfurled, organs stolen, secrets revealed. Most were deformed, cancerous lumps growing in awful places. One, the size of the body marking the child for only five or six years old, looked like an elderly man with sallow skin, creased and divided. The room might have been cold, but then again it might not have been. How could he be sure of anything when he was this numb? Tyler had to take shallow breaths, formalin fumes stinging his eye.

"Holy hell," Sara said. She stood just inside the door, next to the scientist.

"Don't let the boy—" Tyler was too late.

The boy squeezed past Sara. He looked around, trying to grasp what he was seeing, then approached the boy with black hair on the table closest to the door. It looked as if he were being towed. Reeled in. The black-haired boy was partway through dissection, large sections flayed and raw, yellowed fat chunked around grey, bloodless muscles. A tray filled with the dead kid's small intestine sat on a cart next to the body. The kid's face remained, though. They hadn't bothered closing his eyes.

"I'm sorry, Ben," Farris whispered.

"You said you were taking him home."

"You had to know."

"He kept asking to see his mom and dad, but you kept telling me to ask him to stay."

"What you do…this is important work," she said. "You'll understand one day."

The kid reached out a hand and touched the boy's dead face.

"I do, Ms. Kathy."

He looked at Tyler. "Get the recombinant."

"What are you going to do?" Farris whispered as Tyler and her walked to the far end of the lab. Spotlights over each table created pockets of brilliance divided by wedges of darkness. They stopped at a series of steel counters and cabinets lining the wall and the woman presented her face to the genetic sniffer on the center cabinet.

"We have ephermycalthrizine in the lab," she whispered. The light on the lock turned green and she put her hand to the lever, but didn't open it. "For JACKKs. It's new. Buy you years. I can help you, if you'll help me."

Tyler shook his Mark 37 towards the cabinet.

She opened the door and took a steel cylinder out of it, then inserted it into a plunger the size of a baby's arm. Tyler took it from her, held it up and examined it.

"So," he said. "This is the bullet."

"You have no idea what you are doing," she said. "A bullet only kills one person. That boy could kill millions."

"Tell us exactly what the overclock does" Sara said.

"You can't be serious," Farris said.

The Silent Uprising soldiers had moved the four other technicians near the lab door and they were all in the research room again. The boy was standing between Sara and Tyler. Tyler held the recombinant.

"Staern has the key," Tyler said. "What is it? How does it work?"

"Think of a nuclear bomb made out of ebola. The weapon detonates and trillions of genetic stegs are scattered on the wind and bury themselves in every living cell they contact. They replicate and spread from that person like a virus, but a virus that looks for any flaw in your DNA and amplifies it to its terminal. Mortis-models put die-off at twenty to thirty percent of the LCP population if unabated."

Sara held out her hand to Tyler for the recombinant, the glove and crinkled plastic suit spattered with reflections. The other hand held her gun.

The boy was looking at him. Tyler remembered what the boy looked like in his cabin, kneeling in a pool of blood, of Tyler's blood, and the scream he gave when Tyler attacked Eddie. Or in that field after the accident. Mud and a torn jumpsuit. A face contorted with fear and begging misery. Tyler looked at the hacked off arm and felt that the absence wasn't only below the elbow. Hadn't they taken enough? All of them.

Tyler shook his head.

"We had a deal."

"Enough is enough," Tyler said. "Hasn't he had enough?"

The boy kneeling on the side of the van, their orientation sideways, ninety-degrees toward wrong. More blood. Bathing in it. A blood bath.

"You're the one that wants to take him upstairs and blow everyone away."

If you can be counted on for anything, the boy had said.

When Tyler didn't answer, Sara said. "They deserve it. You know that."

"Don't we?"

"Oh, get off it. They kill by the thousands. They protect their own and seize any power they can and they keep it all for themselves. Nobody, not Skimmers, not the average High Laner. Not even an LCP senator can have any."

And there it was. He should have known her crusade wasn't about saving lives any more than his was. He shouldn't have been surprised, but he couldn't deny a part of him was disappointed. "That's what this is about." Tyler said.

"You're talking about the Cullings," Farris said. "Oh my God. You do actually want to end them. I never believed it."

"Shut up," Sara said.

"The only thing keeping us from cannibalism—the smartest civic infrastructure we've ever implemented—and you actually want to end them."

"See?" Sara said to Tyler.

"I never believed it," Farris said.

"They'll never stop. They only care about themselves," Sara said. She shook her open hand.

"No."

"Goddammit! We had a deal!"

"Yeah," the boy said. "You did."

Both Tyler and Sara looked at him. He was twisting the end of a bandage on his arm. When he looked at Tyler, there was both distance and closeness between them. Intense resignation. "You made a promise." But as he said this, he included Sara in his gaze.

"Yeah," Tyler said.

"I did," Sara said.

Deciding to kill someone—it was the kind of thing Tyler had learned was best done with a clear mind. A calm mind. A murder was like a domino. You had to see the full chain to know the price. Later, Tyler would wonder if Sara had even tried measuring that chain before she killed Dr. Farris, Ph.D. in microbiology, genetic engineering and getting shot. He doubted it. If she had, she might have waited a little while. Leave Tyler alive to deal with the next motherfucker upstairs first.

"Anyway, it doesn't matter," Farris started to say. "You cut—"

Sara shot the woman in the face. To Tyler it seemed as if her hair flapped up in slow motion, her skull and every thought she'd ever had misting out the back of it.

"Wait," Tyler shouted.

The other soldiers fired into the backs of the kneeling technicians. Blood and fabric streaked across the floor. And then Tyler felt the rounds tearing into his own guts and ribs. Four of them, at least. Armor piercing, not that it mattered. He fell backwards, the recombinant plunger twirling out of his hand like a baton dropped at the finish line of some race he had known he was in, but had never really thought he could win.

He landed on his back with his head wedged against the door to the lab, like a steel pillow. Black sleep circled his vision.

Sara stood over him, the boy next to her. The boy.

When Sara raised her gun, an MK-9 like Tyler's own, and her hand shook as she aimed at his head, Tyler wondered: she held the gun, but who was pulling the trigger? Somewhere in his Twitcher brain he could tell she had a habit of dropping her wrist when she pulled the trigger, that she might miss his brain, but that this was going to hurt like hell.

He looked at the boy. "I'm sor—"

The gun barked a single shot.

A KILLER

CAUTION, the warning label read. Only hold the incinerator by the handles, the composite handles that hid the inferno between your hands. The vacuums trundled behind, erasing. A scattered few screams and flashing lights. Warnings that would go unnoticed by almost all as they dreamed in their cradles. One second, they were a hero in some syncast, fucking and fighting and handsome, thrilled and erect. The next second, fire between his hands, the whoosh of fuel racing ahead of flame, the swirling containment fields wrapping the body. CAUTION: HOT. Ashes. Dust.

Ben couldn't remember much from Cerebus Gate North, the hit on his head having rattled his memories as much as his body, but he thought it had probably sounded like this. Machine guns arguing back and forth, concrete puffing around them, pinging ricochets off of the steel railings. Ben was counting. Ms. Sara had lost seven of her men in the fighting on the stairs and now they were running to get to Mr. Staern's pen-house. That didn't sound right. Penthouse? Whatever that was.

He tried to decide if his plan was working. Mr. Tyler was going to die anyway, so was Ms. Sara killing him first the best way that all could have gone? Either way, he knew he needed one of them to kill the other before he got to Mr. Staern. Ms. Sara was easier to make do things. Mr. Tyler never did what he asked like the others did.

"That worked out better than I'd expected," Ms. Sara said when the fighting was done and they were climbing to the next level.

"I think he just pretended not to trust people," Ben said.

"Not just that. I'm pretty good at getting what I want. He was easier than that Kibashi girl. Convincing her to set herself on fire in front of her daddy's company without using any drugs or synwarps, now that was something to be proud of. I'm good at getting what I want."

"Me too," Ben said.

***

Blinding, wrenching pain, as if he were gutted from face to crotch. He tried to open his left eye, but it was crusted shut. The Sakanaya dark.

Tyler carefully, carefully put his fingertips to his face. He wiped at his left eye and was able to see through a pink haze. He was lying on the floor in the lab. When he moved his hand to the Sakanaya, twisted metal greeted his fingers. Damn if Sara wasn't a shitty shot, Tyler thought. He kept moving his hand around the side of his face and felt where the bullet had exited. It had been deflected by the cybernetics and came out the side of his skull just in front of his left ear. Brushing his fingers against the wound lit an inferno across his face. Seconds passed before the pain stopped and he could sit up.

First, gripping a protruding power outlet, then a door handle, then the lip of a window, he climbed, dragging his soggy hair along the wall in a crimson arc. A slurping sound sucked from his belly every time he breathed. He looked down. Three of the slugs had already been purged from his guts, he could feel. He reached under his shirt and pulled them out. That meant his JACKK was still working. Had been working. But what was left?

He looked at his watch. 00:00:06:37. Look at those zeroes.

He leaned against the door to that…whatever….behind him, filled with nightmares and in front of him, five dead scientists, a silent scarlet lake reflecting the ceiling lights. This would be the setting of the climax of his life. His final resting place. Surrounded by death. Like the last time he'd thought he would die. The last time he'd tried to die.

And like last time, his death would be in failure. Then, failure as a son. Now, failure as a….what? Kidnapper? Assassin?

Father?

For the first time in maybe ever, Tyler cried.

He was sorry to see Mr. Tyler die. Ben thought he was nicer than he wanted everyone to think. And Ben hadn't wanted to hurt anyone. He'd never wanted to hurt anyone in his life, but they'd hurt him and they weren't going to stop hurting him. It wasn't fair that they had made him be like them. It wasn't fair that they kept trying to use him and make him do things he'd never wanted to do. It wasn't his fault he was a Cull. He hadn't asked to be one. That was Mr. Staern. Well, they were going to get Mr. Staern now. And then Ben would get them all.

First, he'd need to get that recombibent—or whatever it was called — the medicine thingy that would help him kill people. He needed that from Ms. Sara. That was super important.

They stopped at the door to the top floor.

"Stay close to me," Ms. Sara said, her voice stupid and hollow from the suit. "Once they breach the door, we're moving fast. There are security doors in here and we don't want to get trapped behind one."

"You should give me the recombinant," Ben said.

"I'll hold on to it," she said.

The explosion to open the door was quieter than he expected. The scary soldiers with X's on their masks pushed it open and jumped into the hall.

He thought about every person he'd ever killed, every operation he'd led or executed singly. The joyful carnage. Trimming his beard had more meaning to him than the lives he'd ended. How did that happen? When?

Only one life had mattered more than his. No. That was a lie and now, with minutes left, was not the time to lie. Her life didn't matter more than his, but it had mattered. Her death was more. It had changed him.

As would the boy's. The boy. Had he used Sara to try to kill Tyler? Tyler thought about that. Were he in the boy's position, wouldn't he have done the same? The kid was learning. But learning what?

Had Tyler not tried for vengeance, had Eddie Fahrs not died in the fight, had Tyler killed Laser Dick and Glasses and the other SLS assholes that had appeared at his cabin, then let the boy and Fahrs go, where would they all be now? One thing for sure: he wouldn't be on the one-hundred-twentieth floor of the last place on Earth the kid wanted to be, getting the trigger that would vaporize his life into trillions of murdering stegs.

What had he told the boy? For one thing to live, another must die? Tyler was dying. That was foregone. But whose life would his death buy? Or did his life have so little value left as to be worthless? Could his death buy nothing?

00:00:04:14.

He pushed himself off of the wall and wobbled, then stood. He could barely move. What was he thinking?

00:00:04:02.

What had she called it? Ephermycalthrizine. In the lab, she had said. For JACKKs, she had said.

He catapulted one leg in front of the other and somehow made it to the counter without falling.

00:00:03:53.

Ben clasped Ms. Sara's left wrist. It was the hand holding the recombinant plunger, her other hand holding the gun she'd shot Mr. Tyler with.

Dark, raw wooden beams lined the hallway, two rows of cedar columns, carved and magnificent. Warm torches stood sentry in sconces all along the walls, granting the space an amber gentleness that Ben knew wasn't true. The floor was polished mahogany hardwood. It clicked under their boots. Ben had never seen anything like it. Wood!

Two black seams revealed emergency doors that could be closed near the stairs and near the penthouse.

Ben bumped into the back of Ms. Sara and his amputated arm sizzled with pain. She started backing up.

"Dammit," she hissed.

At the end of the hall were two massive wooden doors, each with three panels and standing in front of them was a man. He was big, like Mr. Tyler had been. Black lines traced up his neck and peeked out from under his sleeves. A moment later, when the man started to move faster than any normal person should move, he recognized what they were—the telltale carbon fiber blood vessels of a Twitcher.

***

Vials clinked as they fell out of the cabinets like broken champaign glasses. Empty promises. And how many damn paper towels does a lab need? Tyler moved to the next set of cabinets. Behind him, a dozen open doors gave the cabinets the look of pinned butterflies.

He missed his Sakanaya. It would have been scanning the labels for him, infinitely faster than his one swollen eye trying to focus on the damned small print. Now it was just a piece of broken metal lodged in his face.

Hacking, then sucking a rattling breath, Tyler curled over the counter and vomited chunky blood.

Don't look. It won't help, he thought.

He looked. -00:00:02:35.

He flipped open the next cabinet and saw a vial with the letters EMCT on it. It was small, only 30 millimeters or so. He squinted and tried to focus on the full name: Ephermycalthrizine. A viscous, yellow liquid with silver flecks rocked inside.

There was no way to know what it did or would do. Maybe the scientist had been lying, manipulating him into killing himself. Maybe it wouldn't do anything, his body too far gone for it to help. At this point, did it matter?

The next cupboard had a plunger. He grabbed it and seated the vial into its chamber, closed the cover, put it to his elbow port and pulled the trigger. A single dose snaked into his veins. When the gun had recharged, he pulled the trigger again. If one dose was good, two would be better.

He looked around the wreckage for his bag. The Mark 37 was still slung over his shoulder and the MK-9 was still in his leg holster, but all of the extra magazines in his belt and vest were gone and it looked like the bastards had taken his bag. That left him with one magazine each.

He dropped the plunger and started walking towards the door.

They were dying now. Ben stopped trying to count, but the Twitcher man had shot four of them right away. Bang, bang. Bang, bang. And that was before anyone was even able to move.

Now the Twitcher had closed on another soldier. He slapped the man's rifle up into his own face, then spun him and used him as a shield while shooting at the others. Another two soldiers died trying to move sideways to get around him. The columns in the hallway were the only thing keeping any of them alive, wooden protectors shunting shots off their course.

This wasn't going to work, Ben knew.

"Here." Ms. Sara handed him the recombibet. While shooting with one hand, she unclipped a silver cylinder from her belt with the other. Ben remembered Mr. Tyler using something like that in Cerebus Gate before the semi truck blew up. It frightened him. He didn't want to blow up again.

Ben tightened his grip on the recombibet, then looked at the emergency door they'd just passed under.

The Twitcher's rifle was out of ammo, so he'd dropped it and was now beating the men up really hard. He was smiling. An awful man, just like Mr. Tyler said. Like everyone.

Ben shoved the recombibet into his waist band and started running for the stairwell they'd come through.

Ms. Sara lobbed the grenade, then turned. "No!"

This time felt different. When last Ben was in an explosion like this, whether he wanted to admit it or not, he was grateful to have Mr. Tyler's steel arms wrapped around him, the fatherly warning that this would hurt, the sacrifice of the man's body for the child's. This time, Ben was on his own, the vicious absence of help.

But also the explosion was different. This was a concussion grenade and not a super-exploding grenade, Ben decided.

The explosion threw him to the ground. Furious pain lanced up his amputated arm and wrapped around his eyes like serrated claws. Everything was muted and ringing.

As he stood, he saw Ms. Sara starting to get to her feet, her eyes locked to his. The Twitcher was already back up and all of Ms. Sara's men were crawling and trying to stand.

Ben lurched past the black line of the emergency door, found the alarm panel and slammed his palm into it.

"You little—" The door dropped like a verdict, silencing Ms. Sara's scream.

Was the ringing in his ears from the concussion grenade or guilt? Through the windows in the barrier, he watched Ms. Sara hammer her fists to the gate, watched her face warp with her screams. The fear in that face. Ben felt like he was going to be sick. She was going to die and he'd done it to her. But she was going to kill him. Everyone wanted to kill him or make him kill. Well, they'd have their way. He would kill. All of them. Everyone. Everywhere.

He looked down at the recombibet in his belt. It wasn't there. He spun to look behind him by the alarm panel. Not there. He frantically patted down his pants. Nothing.

Ms. Sara had turned her back to the fire door and was shooting at the Twitcher. Ben stepped up to the window. There were only three men left and her. Three men, the Twitcher, Ms. Sara and the recombibet at her feet.

Twelve minutes! Twelve-mother-fucking-glorious minutes! -00:00:13:58. Look at that. A one in front of the three!

Tyler took the steps three at a time with loping leaps and not a flicker of pain. No after-taste of the ten or eleven bullets he'd eaten in the last two days. And he could hear again! Not just slacker norm hearing, but JACKK hearing. The kind of hearing that told him someone was sitting on the top floor of the stairwell crying and that there were four tired security guards running up the stairs behind him.

A silver bulb, no bigger than Tyler's fist, zipped up the center of the stairwell. It hovered on four flapping wings, a minuscule chain gun for a beak. When it fired, Tyler couldn't help but laugh. It buzzed like a pissed-off hummingbird.

"Oh, c'mon, you guys," Tyler called down the stairs. He fired at the bulb, but missed. "A little birdie to kill me?"

He couldn't remember the last time he'd had this much fun fighting.

Shooting left handed, so he could sight with his left eye, was a lot harder than he'd thought it would be. It took three more bursts before he could nail the drone, but not before it had sent a dozen pellets into him. They burrowed into his arm and cybernetic hand, some skipping off of his rifle, but the kit let him ignore the damage.

Killing the four Staern Life Sciences security officers coming up the stairs behind him was easier. They weren't ready for Tyler's speed or, frankly, his brutality. Odd how men working in the company that invented the Joint Auto-pharmaceutical and Cybernetics Kinesis Kit would have no idea what to expect when facing such a soldier. But there it was. And there they were, four of them, the bodies stacked like cordwood in the stairwell.

He checked their weapons, but confirmed what he'd thought he'd heard in their guns' reports. Mark 41s, not 37s, like his. That meant they were chambered in 8.22mm instead of Tyler's 7.62mm and that the guns would be sync-locked with the guards' cybernetics. He looked at his own rifle. Twelve rounds left, plus his pistol.

Sniffling came from the top of the stairs.

Three flights up, he saw the boy. He was sitting on the landing, his back to the steel door. PRIVATE was printed across it in block letters, then smaller underneath AREN INDUSTRIES GENE SNIFFER X16 EQUIPMENT, NEW YORK, NY. Bullets from the hallway had pimpled this side of the door.

Crusted blood marked the child's face and neck. Raw skin from falling. His amputated arm soaked with blood from the wound that must have reopened. The boy looked at Tyler. Tears tumbling over his round cheeks. Seeing the boy, something broke inside of Tyler.

"I had to try," the boy said. He used the shirt from his shoulder to wipe his nose.

"I know. I would have, too. It was a good plan."

And it had been. Get the lady and the JACKK to try and kill each other and then find a way to wreck the survivor. Enemy of my enemy kind of shit. Yet, Tyler didn't like thinking of this boy as an enemy anymore. When had that happened?

"You don't look good."

"You should talk," Tyler said. He looked at the door, then down the stairs behind him. "Why didn't you run?"

"Where? They'll just blow me up. I don't have the overclock key or the recombinant."

"Maybe you don't need it. They haven't shot you up with the recombinant, activated the stegs. Maybe without that the overclock

won't work either? You could run again. Get out of the LCP." Tyler checked his watch. "I could get you out of the building." And not get Staern? What was he saying? After everything to get here? He wouldn't have time for both.

He whispered, "I could do that for you."

"I need the recombinant," Ben said. He had matched Tyler's whisper, but beneath it were cinder blocks. The kid needed the recombinant. Got it. And Staern had it. That worked out fine for Tyler. Heading the same way as me, kid? Jump on, I'll give you a lift.

Tyler looked through the window in the door. "Staern?"

The boy shook his head. "Everyone's dead. I think the fighting stopped. You don't have to kill Ms. Sara anymore. There's another one, like you, in there."

Another Twitcher, Tyler thought. That complicated things.

The boy sniffed and wiped again at his nose.

"It's been a long couple of days, hasn't it?"

The boy nodded, crying silently.

After a couple of seconds, the boy said, "Mr. Tyler?"

The kid didn't say anything again for a long time. Tyler could tell it took something deep inside of him to find the next words.

"I'm sorry."

Before he knew what he was doing, Tyler had pulled the child up and enfolded him into a hug, his human hand holding the boy's head to his chest, bloody hair splayed between Tyler's fingers. The kid's arms wrapped around him, returning the hug, and Tyler could feel something Skimmers had forgotten, somehow, somewhere over the last hundred years—the touch of family — as if the boy were pouring himself into Tyler, filling him from the inside out with something firmer than love. Steely sunlight. Clarity. Resolve. Purpose. These were words Tyler thought might come close.

The boy filled Tyler with something worth dying for.

His head started to buzz and the world twisted for a moment before settling. He looked at his watch. -00:00:11:13.

"You deserve a chance," Tyler said. "Come on. Let's do some enemy-of-my-enemy kind of shit."

He was going to die. His watch might say ten minutes plus, but Tyler knew his time was up now. There was no way he could beat a healthy JACKK.

"Kid," Tyler said. He was holding the door to the stairwell open, looking through the window of the emergency drop-gate. He could see the Twitcher on the other side typing a code into the panel to raise the gate. "Stay in the stairwell. Be ready to run if…" He let the thought finish itself.

"Okay," the boy said. "And Mr. Tyler?"

Tyler looked at him.

"My name is Ben."

Tyler closed the door.

Eighteen rounds left in the MK-9. Twelve in his rifle. Thirty prayers.

The first sign of death was the smell of burning flesh. A smell Tyler knew well. The gate crawled upwards, as if it understood the ridiculous melodrama it was a bit player in, building tension between two stars. Until the windows had raised too far, they evaluated one another as if seeing in a mirror for the first time. Is this what I look like? Although this Twitcher had opted for total optic replacement, where Tyler had wanted only one, a choice he was regretting at this moment as the smoke made his natural eye water. This Twitcher was younger than Tyler, stronger. He looked to be three or four centimeters taller and maybe twenty kilos heavier. It wasn't fat. Cybernetic studs poked from his forehead under a beanie cap. He looked insane — the ragged smile not helping.

Tyler never took his eye off of the Twitcher, never blinked, despite the burn. Now was not a time for blinking. Normally, Tyler knew, striking first and fast was the best strategy, but not with a Twitcher. He'd never fought one before, but he knew the rules would be different. This man would be faster than Tyler. There was no advantage that he could think of that would help him through this.

"It feels good, doesn't it?" the Twitcher said once they could speak. He tapped one of the steel carotids in his neck.

"Not anymore, no."

The man finished reloading his sidearm, holstered it and rested his hands on another one of those Mark 41s. He'd probably shoot from the hip, Tyler knew. It would be an arc from low right to high left. If Tyler could side-step and roll, he could dodge the low shots and go under the high ones.

"Am I going to be your first?"

"What's that?"

"The first fight you lose since getting JACKK'd?"

Tyler smirked.

"Nah," he said. "I think I've probably lost every day I've lived."

"Is that philosophy or something?"

"Sure."

Tyler would have to shoot twice before spinning and again immediately after to keep the Twitcher from getting a second salvo in.

"The Cull dead? I'm not supposed to kill the Cull, but he ran when the fighting got started and I haven't seen him since."

"Yeah, he is."

"Bummer. They didn't tell me why you all were doing this."

"Philosophy. Or something," Tyler said. "We don't have a lot of time. Shall—"

Dammit, the Twitcher was fast. Tyler had thought he would at least see a flinch or something, but one second he was talking and the next the Mark 41 was vomiting bullets. Tyler slid to his right, firing his own rifle twice, missing, then crouched and spun back to his left under the arc of rounds. While crouching, he swept his foot towards the Twitcher's legs and at the same time fired two more rounds. The Twitcher skipped over the sweep-kick, but took the two rounds in the gut. Tyler heard the demoralizing foop of a melmoth vest under his shirt.

For fuck's sake. Would nothing ever be easy?

Ben went up on his tiptoes to look through the window. They were fighting now. He could hear the guns, but couldn't see a whole lot and what he did see was more motion and blur than understood.

That was a lot of bodies in there, it was good the hallway was so wide. Mr. Tyler would have room to move. Ben could see Ms. Sara. Her head was on her neck crooked, in a way that Ben had never seen before, so that she looked kind of like a dead owl. He was glad she was dead. All of them.

Then he saw the recombinant. Mr. Tyler had told him to stay in here, but Ben was tired of other people telling him what to do, of hoping other people would protect him and take care of him. It wasn't very far from the door. Maybe...

Distance. Maybe if he got some distance, he would have time to think. Tyler stepped around one of the wood columns, then fired three times as he raced to the next column. Compared to the other guy's gluttonous gun, Tyler sounded like a miser with his shots.

Tyler felt a bullet enter and leave his left biceps, then finally rest inside his torso, just past the ribs. Rigid heat riddled his chest.

He dropped to his knees and slid behind the column for cover, wooden splinters raining over him, falling inside his shirt. He fired two more shots from behind the column, one of them missing wide, but the other finding the Twitcher's arm.

"Thirty-seven," the Twitcher shouted. He fired at Tyler again. The edges of the column were being chewed away as if a flock of furious woodpeckers had taken the column to task. "I've been shot thirty-seven times now since getting JACKK'd and I've never felt a single one. Isn't that the coolest thing ever?"

No, Tyler thought. Not. Fucking. Cool. Because he was feeling all of that bullet the Twitcher had just sent his way.

When he heard the click of the Twitcher's gun, he rolled out from behind the column and sprinted towards the man, firing the final three rounds from his rifle. Two Silent Uprising bodies lay between them. The Twitcher let the rounds hit his vest and sprinted towards Tyler. Just before they reached each other, the Twitcher kicked the head of one of the bodies. It exploded like a water balloon splaying shrapnel made of bone, brains and tissue across Tyler's face. A blood veil. Before he could blink away the gore, the Twitcher jackhammered the butt of his rifle into the side of Tyler's skull.

Ben eased open the stairwell door. Mr. Tyler wasn't going to win. The other guy was really beating on his face with the rifle and it looked like Mr. Tyler couldn't stand very well.

He ran for the recombinant. Not three steps from the door, he slipped on someone's intestines laying in the hallway like a tripwire. He landed on his amputated arm and screamed.

Skipper Johnson. That was a name Tyler hadn't thought of in a long time. The Red Lithium Big S1m had killed by smashing his face against a pylon seven or eight times. S1m's swollen girth glistening with sweat. Skip had been the closest thing to a friend Tyler had in the Lithiums.

As the butt of the Mark 41 dropped again, Tyler wondered if this is what it felt like for Skip. No matter how big the nanocellotics could make your muscles, they couldn't insert a cushion between your brain and the inside of your skull. So when the Twitcher's rifle slammed into Tyler's face over and over, it wasn't just the broken cranium that hurt, it was his grey matter playing chicken with the inside of that cranium that really screwed things up. The world sang from under cotton balls. Muffled nonsense.

The Twitcher was talking to him. He was smiling and his lips were saying words, but Tyler couldn't put them together. Something about seeing ghosts.

Then Tyler saw the boy. He was laying on the floor next to the woman. This seemed bad, but Tyler'd be damned if he could remember why. Something about the silver plunger by the woman. The thing the boy was reaching for. Reaching. There was something Tyler should reach for. The Twitcher wasn't looking at Tyler right now, he was looking at the boy and that meant now was the time, but for what?

They say there is such a thing as muscle memory. The Chinese call it mushin. No-mindedness. Later, not much later, only minutes, Tyler would think maybe that's what happened. His hand found his sidearm, pulled it free of the holster, pushed it to the Twitcher's chest and pulled the trigger so fast it sounded like an automatic weapon. Melmoth vest or not, at this range it didn't matter. The splatter rounds tore into the Twitcher, blooming beneath his skin.

The Twitcher coughed, slapped away Tyler's gun and went at him with a thunderstorm of kicks, elbows and punches. He blocked some, ate others. The Twitcher caught one of Tyler's punches and hyper-extended the arm in an elbow lock, breaking bones. More punches. Tyler choked on a lost tooth. Fell backwards.

On his back, he spotted his pistol and rolled twice until he was up against a column and able to scoop up the pistol. The Twitcher chased him while he rolled, kicking at Tyler between steps. Tyler came up on a knee and railed out with the MK-9.

"Got you, motherfu—"

Tyler stopped just before squeezing the trigger. Somehow, somewhere, while Tyler was picking up the pistol, the Twitcher had picked up the boy, dangling, thrashing. A desperate shield.

"Don't," the boy screamed.

The Twitcher's life gurgled in his voice as he said, "Wouldn't want to hurt the—"

Tyler didn't let him finish. He lunged forward and scooped the Twitcher's legs together, spearing his shoulder into the kid and pushing him into the Twitcher's perforated chest as they hit the ground. Both child and Twitcher grunted. The kid slipped the man's arm over his face, then slid away.

And then it was something more than fighting. It was more than tactics and timing. The Twitcher was good, had been trained by the best, had the best sync-skills installed, but it couldn't compare. It couldn't. It wasn't the same as a life with the Red Lithiums, fighting for them, then fighting to escape them. It wasn't the same as a life after the Red Lithiums, living on hollow streets selling whatever you had to offer — willing or not — to whomever was awake and buying. And it wasn't the same as six years of JACKK life, murdering at a national level.

He climbed on top of the Twitcher, landing meteors in the man's face. The Twitcher bucked and rolled so he was on top, Tyler beneath, but Tyler pushed the man's face away. He wrapped a leg behind the man's neck and cinched it under the knee of his other leg, forming a triangle choke. He could feel the carotid sheaths dig into his thighs. The man grunted and tried to stand, but Tyler rocked his weight and brought them back to the ground. Tyler used

his broken arm to hold the man's head and started punching with his flesh hand. The bullet buried in his side scraped against a rib with every heave. He broke the man's nose, then his cheek bone under the right eye, then the man's left Sakanaya cracked and sank into the socket, then the left cheek bone, then the brow ridge over the right Sakanaya. The Twitcher tried to block the punches with his one free hand, but Tyler batted it down and continued with machine insistence. With every punch, the skull gave way to jagged mush, the bones in no way designed to withstand Tyler's JACKK. He could feel his own hand collapsing under the onslaught. But wasn't that what he'd been created for? Wasn't this his only value?

When the Twitcher's face was concave, an abstract of a man, Tyler stopped. He lay gasping, staring at the copper scrollwork on the ceiling.

Tyler couldn't help himself. "Did you feel that?" he whispered.

The boy offered Tyler his hand to help pull him up.

Tyler's pain went vertical with him. He looked at his watch. -00:00:04:06. The sixty-second fight had taken seven of his last minutes. Already the swelling in his left elbow made it impossible to bend his arm more than ten or twenty degrees and his right hand was a gnarled mess of digits and porcupining bones. He probed the gunshot in his side. Breathing was hard, but he didn't think he would die before his four minutes were up.

He drew his MK-9. Three rounds left.

They had done a number on Malcolm Staern's hallway. Thirteen of the Silent Uprising soldiers lay dead, some shot to hell, others bludgeoned. And there, Sara. She'd been shot and trampled in the fight and what was left twisted at odd angles. Iron colored hair bubbled out of a tear in her environment suit's hood.

"For something to live," the boy said, "something else has to die, right? Isn't that what you told me?"

"At least she died for something." If Tyler owed her anything, he owed her credit for that.

"She was going to use me to kill the High Laners she didn't like, she said."

"I didn't say it was something worthy."

132

"I didn't say it wasn't."

Phosphorous pain flashed behind Tyler's eye, in rhythm with his pulse. It was getting hard to hold his head up.

"I thought you were going to shoot me," the boy said. "To get that Twitcher. I thought you wouldn't care and would shoot through me."

"Never." Tyler rested his hand on the boy's head, his hair gelled with blood and soot. "Not ever."

He guided the child towards Staern's suite. "Let's finish this."

When Tyler did finally die, in those terminal seconds, he would think back to this moment, his mutilated body heaving against Malcolm Staern's doors and feel this was the happiest he had ever been. A copper joy sparking through him. Hard fought. A reward years in the earning, but earned it was. It was earned.

"He's not here," the boy said.

The fuck he wasn't. They'd checked. Sara had said they had access to his schedule, that they had people watching him.

He panned his MK-9 across the room again. The ceiling soared seven meters over their heads, with glowing iridescent panels. Two walls were nothing but glass, Elia's lights sprawling to the edge of the earth. In the recessed center of the room, a ring of black leather couches circled a holopad projecting the death scene in the hallway. A half-drunk glass of wine next to it.

"He's not here," the boy said again, sitting on the steps leading down toward the holopad. An odd laughing-sob slipped out as he sat.

"He's here," Tyler said. "You don't use a Twitcher for a body guard unless there's a body to guard."

Then the wall to their left beeped. What Tyler'd thought was a decorative wall panel betrayed itself as an elevator. Staern was chicken-shitting outta' here. The holopad had shown him enough.

Tyler hobbled toward the elevator, the boy following.

Before the door was even half open, Tyler shoved his gun through the crack, sighted on the helicopter thirty or thirty-five meters away. Rich fucks. Should have known Staern'd have his own Avalon Six ready to skirt him off like the crotch wart he was. Slip into the night. Those two GE CT-26 Thrusters and a whisper-silent rotor only helped if you got in the air, though.

Malcolm Staern was climbing into the Avalon, one hand grabbing a handle to pull himself up, a heavy nylon bag in the other.

Tyler fired twice. The first round shattered the cockpit window, the second the pilot's head.

The display on the back of Tyler's gun read "1." One bullet left. One head left to shoot. That math added up just fine.

The wind up here was something Tyler hadn't expected. Arrows along the perimeter of the landing pad lit up and rotated as the wind shifted direction, numbers ticking up and down tracking its speed. From here, Tyler could see the known world. For better or worse. He almost felt he could reach up and touch the Veil, it's cotton glow reflecting city lights. It wasn't a word he used often, but Tyler thought it might even be beautiful.

Ben huddled behind Tyler, clinging to the pouches on his belt as they stepped off of the elevator. The gravel roof crunched.

"Three girls," Malcolm Staern called. He set down his bag and began walking towards Tyler and the boy.

The helicopter sensed the dead pilot and cycled down its rotors.

"That's how many daughters he had. He was a good pilot."

"Suddenly we care?"

Disgusted, Staern shook his head. "Trust me when I tell you, this is not going to go the way you think it is."

He looked different in person than in the newscasts. He was smaller with a brave, smooth scalp, bright with clipped hair buoying it on the sides and back. He walked with a steady confidence, as if no matter where he was going, he set the schedule, set the route. There wasn't any fear that Tyler could sense. There wasn't an acknowledgement that his life had already ended. He must know. Why wasn't he afraid?

"Tyler Samson. As I live and breathe."

"Not for long."

"We'll see. Even so, I am glad you're here. The Twitcher That

Walked. We never did figure out how you survived Liberty Heights or what happened in that tower. How did that go so wrong?"

"Give me the key," Ben screamed. He moved out from behind Tyler.

"Benjamin," Staern said. He smiled at the boy. "Son, it is good to have you home."

"Don't call him 'son,'" Tyler said.

"I don't suppose I can convince you to come back to us, Ben?"

Tyler's watch beeped. Three minutes. "Give him the key."

"He's been controlling you, you know," Staern said to Tyler. "All of this. None of it has been your own will or idea. We built a pheromone simplex into the Cull that would allow him to convince people to take him in, keep passing him from one unit to the next to help spread the steg. You've been gumped this entire time."

"Not Tyler," the boy said. "It doesn't work on him."

That firmness within Tyler — that something the boy had filled him with in the stairwell — it shifted, not seismically, but enough to open a gap. Smeared edges of confidence started slipping and Tyler wondered if it might be true. Had the boy played Tyler this entire time? Made him dance? He thought about those moments the kid had wailed impotently: in the jeep begging Tyler to turn around, in the hospital when he asked Tyler to kill Sara. He remembered the light-headedness, the lost time on his watch. Was the boy telling the truth? What Tyler had thought were symptoms of his JACKK wearing down, could they have been symptoms of it fighting off this simplex thing?

"Interesting. That'll make things harder," Staern said. "Maybe you've already discovered this, Ben, but I find it difficult to know if someone is doing what I ask because they want to or because they are compelled to."

Tyler understood, but he could tell the boy was confused.

"You didn't think I wouldn't take that power for myself, did you," Staern said. "I'm convinced this simplex is more important than your steganography."

"Enough," Tyler said. "The overclock key." His gun was getting heavy. His gun! His body was giving up on him, although who could blame it? But time was short. The boy had the recombinant.

Get him the overclock key and the kid would be able to live free. Run. Disappear into the city and use this pheromone whatever to convince people to take care of him — something Tyler could have used when he was the boy's age. How would his own life have turned out if he'd had just one person offer him a bed, a nutrient sac, even a smile when he was running the streets at Ben's age? Well, the boy would have that. He'd make them offer it. And if the boy had, in fact, forced Tyler on this whole mission through some chemical persuasion and none of this had been Tyler's idea…well, then his life would end the same way it had been lived…as a tool.

"The overclock key? But it's useless," Stern said. "You cut out the transponder. We couldn't activate it if we wanted."

Tyler wanted to laugh. The kid hadn't been in any danger since they'd cut off his arm? He could have run any time after that. No need for the recombinant. No need to be here on this roof now.

But Tyler had a need, didn't he? Hustle the kid along and then finish what he came here for.

"Alright, kid," Tyler said. "Time for you to—"

"Good," the kid said. He fitted the recombinant to his left arm's IV port. Before either Tyler or Staern could react, the boy had pulled the trigger.

Both men shouted, "No!"

Tyler's watch beeped. -00:00:02:00.

When he had dreamed about this moment, Tyler had thought, after everything, when only minutes remained, that the world would make more sense. That by now he would be forcing it to make sense. He was the one with the gun, after all. He had the target, the man responsible for so much of his miserable life at the sharp end of the barrel and, surprise, surprise, the boy-weapon he'd planned to blow up in the act no longer needed to die. In fact, Tyler found himself desperate to keep the boy-weapon from blowing up at all. It had seemed he might be able to do two meaningful things with his final minutes: save a child and kill a monster. Now, with the recombinant ambling through the kid's arteries, gleefully tripping poisonous genetic markers left and right, Tyler's world was as upside-fucked as ever.

"Why?" Pathetic, but the best he could do.

"You were right, Mr. Tyler," the boy said. "People are awful." He gulped a shuddering breath, then knelt on the gravel rooftop. He looked at his amputated arm and said, "Everybody hurts each other. I've never met anyone nice. Not you. Not Ms. Sara. Not the doctors who made Eric sick and wouldn't let him see his mom and dad. Not the food vendor. Not even the man I gave food to. Do you know what he said when I handed it to him? 'Fuck off.' Well, I am, and everyone else is too. We're all going to fuck off and die. Starting in the High Lanes. You were right, Mr. Tyler."

"Shoot him," Malcolm said. There was the fear. Cutting.

"You were free."

"I was never going to be free." The boy looked at Tyler and there was a swallowing void behind the boy's eyes where something akin to hope used to be. It wasn't hopelessness that had replaced it. It was worse. Apathy.

"Kill him," Staern said. Tyler felt light headed. "If he leaves here, we'll never find him. He'll go from family to family hiding and nobody will ever betray him or know why they're helping him and then they'll die and their neighbors will die and their neighbors' neighbors."

Tyler had to lower his gun from pointing at Staern, it was too heavy.

"High Laners, Tyler. Everything good. Everything we've built and saved. Dead."

"Stop it," the boy said.

For a second, the sounds of traffic and wind muted and Tyler couldn't keep his eye open, then the dizziness passed.

"He'll be killing High Laners. Do you realize what will happen? Do you recognize the edge our nation sits on? How the resource gap has driven us to this edge? High Laners are the only people keeping civilization alive, Tyler. Engineers and doctors. Innovators. Everything good."

"Stop using the simplex on him," the boy said to Staern.

Was that what was happening? He wanted to slap his face, try to wake from this fog, but he couldn't find the strength.

"Good," Tyler said. "That's what you call this? What you built the boy to do? The Cullings?"

"This is what you wanted, Mr. Tyler," the boy said. "You've been right all along."

"This is bigger than you or the boy now. Bigger than some stupid revolution," Staern said. "What we do—what I and the boy...and you — we balance the scales. Everywhere around you there is good that needs to be protected. You've seen it your whole life."

"I've seen murder."

"From people like you, Mr. Staern," Ben said.

"You've seen necessary suffering to save the greater good. But you've also seen joy, Tyler, you've only blinded yourself to it. Passing through the city you probably saw families coming home from work. They do that to care for each other...out of joy."

"A Skimmer would kill for a job."

"And they'd be miserable with one. Half of the High Laners dread their mornings, but that's their sacrifice. Out of love. For their families. This nation. For the last hope of civilization."

"How about a Skimmer, you fuck? They give their lives."

"Some. Yes. Few, but some. Every Culling needs fewer sacrifices. We are so close, Tyler. And what do they get in trade? A life of joy unlike anything I will ever experience. Not just numbness, but true bone-marrow joy."

"They get loneliness." Tyler saw himself, seven and half naked, stealing from his neighbor, Jackson Wallace's nutrient portions because his mother had ignored him during her last relapse. He thought of the fear of loneliness. The fear of weakness after fleeing Big S1m the first time. What he'd been forced to trade to predators of all kinds in order to stay alive.

"If you let this boy leave here, he will kill everyone near him. We'll never be able to find and stop him. He's already infecting you and I."

Tyler could feel both of them staring at him, their chemical will crashing against him. His watch beeped again. One minute. Time was moving too fast. They were triggering his JACKK.

"They've used you just like they used me, Mr. Tyler," the boy said. "They made you do things you hated."

"Tyler," Staern's voice dropped to almost a whisper. "Tyler, in

any life, we will only ever be given one chance to do the most important thing we can for someone else. This is yours. Please. I'm begging you. Stop Ben. Don't let him ruin all of those lives. Tens of millions. Men, women. Children. Don't let him burn the LCP into ashes. Please, Tyler."

Tyler thought about the woman buying olives at the train station, the vet tech at the farm and her little boy. He thought about the boy walking along the river with his father. Hand in hand. Where were they now? Eating dinner together? With a sister, maybe? Getting pajamas on for bedtime. The kinds of things he played at in syncasts as a child. Was Tyler going to let this boy kill all of them? Sure, maybe not directly with his own steganography, but if what Staern said was true, they would sure as shit die in the aftermath as the High Lanes collapsed. Or they'd wish they had when the Midlands broke through.

"He made you a JACKK," Ben said. "Killed you in six years."

Tyler's watch beeped again. Thirty seconds.

"Killed," Staern looked at the boy. "We saved this man's life. Killed him in six years? We gave him six years he wouldn't have had out on the street. All alone. A Skimmer. What did you weigh when you signed with us? Sixty kilos? He was weeks from dying."

Could he do both? Could Tyler shoot the boy and still get Malcolm? Maybe throw him off the roof? He raised the gun to waist level, bobbing it between the kid and Staern. Even that was painful. He couldn't take a step, much less chase Staern across the landing pad.

Was he honestly going to kill this kid? But how could he honestly let him go? Tears stung his eye. He wanted to scream. This wasn't how it was supposed to be. Simple revenge. That's all he'd wanted. One fucking thing that was only his. How the fuck did he let the kid get under his skin like this? How did he let the boy become something more than a weapon?

He had to admit that Staern was right, though. The world wasn't the shit-hole Tyler had always said it was. Those first years running with the Lithiums, with Mickey and Pillsbury and Grubs, hell, even Crupps, the shit they'd pulled, laughs they'd had, that was real. The way Big S1m held his daughter. That was real.

What was the kid supposed to do, though? One thing he could have done, Tyler raged, was not inject the fucking recombinant. God dammit! Maybe that's what life is, a series of consequences for choices. After all, nobody forced Tyler to join the Red Lithiums. Nobody forced him to get JACKK'd. Maybe the boy needed to suffer his own consequence now. Tyler couldn't let this kid leave here, killing. A killer. The boy had made his choice. He'd left Tyler none.

"This is what Ben will destroy. Even Skimmers love each other. You are only here because your mother gave up two years of being under so she could care for you until you could be ported. Love. For you, Tyler. A sacrifice she was willing to make for a greater good."

"Mr. Tyler," the boy whispered, "he killed her. He killed your mom."

The belly of that lie sliced open and out of it tumbled a truth Tyler couldn't hide from any longer. All of this, the murderous child, the dead revolutionaries, the man begging for his life, his dead mother, all of it was Tyler's fault. At no point in his last twenty-seven years had he even once considered another person as anything more than a tool, a path to get what he wanted. And where had that path brought him?

His fault. All of it. Most especially her death. Hers.

He felt the weight of his gun, the weight of the single shot left.

His watch beeped. Fifteen seconds.

"Ben," Tyler said. A name. At the end, a son deserved to be named. He stared at Malcolm Staern as he said, "I lied to you. My mom didn't get Culled when I was a kid. It happened two years ago. In Liberty Heights. And it wasn't me hiding in the oven. It was her."

He turned to the boy.

"I was the Cull."

Through the blood roaring in his head, the gunshots in his temples, Tyler could hear sirens approaching, could smell the Veil-filtered air, glassy and cool. The wind chilled his fevered sweat.

"Your mother..." Staern let the words fail.

"Just remember this one thing," Tyler said. "In life, you can't call back a bullet."

And then, for the first time ever, Tyler did something for another person out of a feeling almost akin to love.

He shot Malcolm Staern.

The boy stood over him. He didn't remember falling. His vision was pinwheeling. The boy helped him to lean up against a ventilation pipe so he was facing the elevator.

"My right pocket," Tyler whispered.

Ben pulled out Eddie Fars's credit chip.

"And this." Tyler unlatched his watch, his fingers fat and stupid at the clasp.

Ben took the watch and buckled it around his own wrist. "Thank you," he said.

"You're on your own now."

"I know."

"You'll always be alone." Tyler couldn't stem the tears. "I don't think we were meant to be alone."

"I'll never be alone. Until I am. When it's over."

Tyler tried to nod, but once his head fell forward he couldn't lift it again. He slumped sideways and lay there. He could see the back of Ben walking towards the elevator and he listened to the sirens in the city below and he felt the piercing gravel in his cheek, the lazy grind of the bullet against his ribs with his last breaths. He heard his watch's alarm go off, the boy in the elevator looking at him, waiting for the doors to close.

Tyler Lyle Samson, six years, three months and two days after becoming a JACKK for the LCP military, let out a final sigh.

The elevator exited the building at a private entrance. Privacy. All of that money and power and Mr. Staern used it to make sure he could be alone. Ben walked out onto the street under SLS tower and chose a random direction to start walking. Most of the towers here were for companies, Ben knew, but some of the storefronts had residences above them.

LCP police screamed down the street toward Staern Tower. Ben began running and turned at the next intersection. He was looking behind him and didn't see the man holding two overloaded nylon bags, trying to use his thumb sensor to unlock his store's front door. Ben collided into the man's backside.

"Easy, son," the man said. His voice sounded like Mr. Tyler's, deep and dry, but warmer. Kinder. "Lots of commotion tonight," he said.

Ben said he was sorry for bumping into the man. He met the man's eyes and tried to smile.

"You look terrible," the man said.

"I could use help," Ben admitted. "I don't know anyone around here."

The man smiled at him, then grimaced. He put one of the bags down and rubbed at his chest.

"Come on in," he said. He took Ben's hand and walked with him toward the door. "I'm not feeling too great myself suddenly. Let's get away from this ruckus and I'll get you cleaned up. I know lots of people around here."

SERIOUSLY.
THANK YOU.

Everyone says it, but I doubt they mean it as much as I mean it right now. This story was important to me and I appreciate anyone spending time in the world. I hope you feel uneasy right now, after the story. Like things weren't buttoned up the way you had hoped they would be. Maybe you're still thinking about it. If so, please consider leaving an honest and fair review wherever you bought the book, or telling your friends about it. Reviews are the lifeblood of authors. I would love it if you'd help other readers find books they might enjoy chewing over or stay away from books they might not.

Thank you so much for supporting my work.

www.kalebschadauthor.com

GET THE
TWITCHER SKETCHBOOK
FOR FREE!

Get a downloadable PDF of the Twitcher Sketchbook for free. Join the mailing list and get early access to new releases, exclusive art, deleted scenes and sneak peeks at projects in development.

kalebschadauthor.com/join

Thank you for reading!
Kaleb Schad

ABOUT THE AUTHOR

Kaleb Schad lives in Green Bay, Wisconsin, working as a creative director by day and writes and illustrates fantasy and science fiction stories by night (mornings, too). He spent his early childhood years in the heart of God's country—called northwestern Montana by some—then, moved to Wisconsin in his early teens. Nobody calls Wisconsin God's country. He did have a boss call it the armpit of the country once. He laughed. Then cried. But it is where he met the most amazing woman basically on the face of the planet and she gave him the two most amazing sons on the face of the planet. So there is that.

www.ingramcontent.com/pod-product-compliance
Lightning Source LLC
Chambersburg PA
CBHW070334130626
46556CB00007B/2864